CW00693650

THE CAMDEN SPIRITUALIST

A Penny Green Mystery Book 12

EMILY ORGAN

Copyright © 2022 by Emily Organ

This edition © Emily Organ 2024

emilyorgan.com

Emily Organ has asserted her right under the Copyright, Designs and
Patents Act 1988 to be identified as the author of this work.

All characters and events in this publication, other than those clearly in the
public domain, are fictitious and any resemblance to real persons, living or
dead, is purely coincidental.

ISBN 978-1-7396766-1-2

This book is copyright material and must not be copied, reproduced,
transferred, distributed, leased, licensed or publicly performed or used in any
way except as specifically permitted in writing by the publisher, as allowed
under the terms and conditions under which it was purchased or as strictly
permitted by applicable copyright law. Any unauthorised distribution or use
of this text may be a direct infringement of the author's and publisher's
rights and those responsible may be liable in law accordingly.

THE PENNY GREEN SERIES

Limelight
The Rookery
The Maid's Secret
The Inventor
Curse of the Poppy
The Bermondsey Poisoner
An Unwelcome Guest
Death at the Workhouse
The Gang of St Bride's
Murder in Ratcliffe
The Egyptian Mystery
The Camden Spiritualist

CHAPTER 1

"Welcome, ladies and gentlemen, to the Theatre Royal Drury Lane!"

The audience responded with a round of applause. Once it had subsided, the grey-whiskered man on the stage continued. "Allow me to introduce myself to those who are unfamiliar with the name Professor Mortimer. I am a scientist. For many years, I studied the remarkable elements of this earth. But these days I devote my work to a much higher cause. The world of spiritualism."

He paused to allow his words to sink in. His wavy grey hair extended beyond his collar and he wore a double-breasted black velvet jacket over a pair of black breeches.

"Joining me on stage this evening is a girl who requires no introduction at all. However," he raised a finger, "for the benefit of anybody here who hasn't heard of her – and I doubt there are many," he grinned, "her name is Elizabeth Shelley."

This statement was met with further applause. Professor Mortimer drew his hands behind his back and smiled as he waited for the noise to subside.

"Her history, as you know, is quite remarkable. A young waif, she was abandoned at St Pancras Workhouse. She was schooled there, as every young child at the workhouse is these days, but her lessons did not go to plan. As the schoolmistress attempted to instruct her young charges in letters and numbers, they heard mysterious tapping sounds coming from the corner of the classroom. Upon further investigation, no one could determine their source.

"As time went by, the regularity of these sounds intensified. And it wasn't just tapping sounds. Before long, objects were witnessed to be moving entirely of their own accord! The items were small to begin with – a piece of chalk and a writing slate – but then larger items began to move – a desk, followed by an entire bench with eight children seated upon it!

"After a while, these unexplained phenomena manifested themselves in other parts of the building. In the children's dormitory, gaslights swung on their fittings, bedsheets were pulled off unsuspecting children and beds moved around the room! Naturally, the children grew extremely fearful, and a priest was called in to examine what many believed to be the actions of a malevolent spirit. However, further investigations revealed something crucial. The only person present during every unexplained incident happened to be Elizabeth Shelley."

The audience around me in the upper circle remained quiet, seemingly entranced by the story, even though many had almost certainly heard it before. There was no doubt that Professor Mortimer was a proficient storyteller, but I struggled to be convinced.

"I'd like you to write a review of the young medium, Elizabeth Shelley," the editor of the *Morning Express* newspaper, Mr Sherman, had asked me a few days previously. "She's causing quite a stir with her abilities, and our readers would like to hear what happens at her shows."

"I'm not someone who believes in psychic powers," I replied.

"You don't need to believe in them, Mrs Blakely. Just write a review of what you see. Perhaps she may convince you."

"I doubt it, sir."

I had accepted the commission as an act of loyalty to my former employer, hoping the next request would focus on a topic that interested me a little more.

Professor Mortimer continued his story. "The priest questioned Miss Shelley and she claimed the cause of the trouble was a spirit who went by the name of Sally Moulin," he said. "It seemed this spirit had chosen her in order to communicate with the land of the living, and Miss Shelley was extremely afraid of her.

"I became involved in this curious case a little over three years ago, in the summer of 1882. A mutual friend of the priest alerted me, knowing I possessed a profound interest in spiritualism and the supernatural. My immediate response was one of concern for this poor young girl who had found herself burdened with such a remarkable ability.

"Upon meeting her, I was struck by her maturity and serenity, in the face of what must have been extremely trying circumstances. I took her into my Camden home – my priority being to help her control the spirit of Sally Moulin."

I felt myself growing impatient, keen to see what Elizabeth Shelley was capable of. She had become a real sensation within the past year, yet I wasn't exactly sure why. Whatever she intended to demonstrate this evening, I knew it would be trickery; however, it concerned me that so many members of the audience seemed prepared to believe her powers were genuine.

"Ladies and gentlemen!" he called out. "Please welcome to the stage, Miss Elizabeth Shelley!"

Applause rang out around me, and I tapped my hands together, aware that it would be churlish to show no sign of appreciation at all.

A slight girl, who appeared younger than her fifteen years, walked out onto the stage. She wore a plain blue dress and her mouse-brown hair was tied in a long plait.

Professor Mortimer rested a hand on her shoulder as she stood next to him. "Please be aware, ladies and gentlemen, that you may hear unexpected noises or even witness objects moving around, as if transported by an invisible hand. I urge you to remain calm at all times. The spirits are often more afraid than you are! I appreciate that you may feel alarmed at certain points during the show, but please rest reassured that there is nothing in the least to worry about."

The curtain behind him lifted to reveal a three-walled wooden booth. Within the booth was a simple wooden chair. Professor Mortimer placed his hand on Miss Shelley's back and guided her over to the chair. He gestured for her to sit and, as she did so, pulled a number of ribbons from his pocket.

"For the benefit of the sceptics and doubters," he said, "I shall now tether Miss Shelley to this chair so she cannot stand until the end of the performance."

We watched as he tied her ankles to the legs of the chair with the ribbons. Then she joined her hands together around the back of the chair so he could also tie them together. "And just to be certain," he continued, "I shall now place a silk pillowcase over Miss Shelley's head. She will be able to breathe perfectly normally, but it will deprive her of her senses."

I wasn't sure how a thin pillowcase could completely deprive someone of their senses, but the spectacle was complete when the professor pulled the red silk pillowcase over her face and her head slumped forward, as if she had suddenly passed into a trance. Then he stepped back and pulled a red velvet curtain across the front of the booth with a flourish, the brass rings jangling on the pole.

"I must insist on complete and utter silence as Miss Shelley manifests the spirit of Sally Moulin!" he called out. "Please remain silent during the proceedings. If there is any noise or distraction, the show will have to be halted, and I'm sure you would all be sorely disappointed if that were to happen."

The lights dimmed as the professor stepped to one side of the stage, plunging the curtained booth into darkness. Then a spotlight appeared on a curtain on the other side of the stage from the booth.

There was a long pause – so long that I grew impatient – and then came a slight, yet discernible, movement from behind the curtain. The woman next to me gave a nervous giggle.

"Who goes there?" Professor Mortimer called out.

There was no reply. Instead, the curtain shifted again.

"Show yourself!" he commanded.

The curtain moved again, this time a little more vigorously.

"Don't be shy! We are all waiting to hear from you. We're ready to accept whatever you have to say. Step out and show yourself!"

The curtain shook so vigorously that I wondered if it would fall from its fittings. There was something rather amateurish about the spectacle, my toes curled a little with embarrassment.

Suddenly, the curtain was flung to one side and gasps sounded all around me. A girl in a long white robe stood there, illuminated by an eerie green light, her hair long and loose. It was difficult to discern her features, but she was of the same height and stature as Miss Shelley. In fact, I had no doubt that it *was* Miss Shelley. She had clearly escaped her ribbons and walked around the back of the curtain before loosening her hair, pulling on a robe and emerging on the opposite side of the stage.

"Tell me your name," said the professor.

"Sally Moulin." Her voice was rough and raspy; presumably an effect Miss Shelley adopted to make it sound otherworldly.

"Who are you, Sally Moulin?"

"I am no one."

"But surely you must be someone."

The girl didn't answer. Instead, she slowly raised her hands until they were held out in front of her, her palms facing the audience. "He's here," she announced.

"Who?"

"Joey."

"*Joey?*"

"Joey Grimaldi."

She was referring to Joseph Grimaldi, an actor who had been famous for playing a clown at this theatre. It was rumoured that his ghost haunted the place. A long discussion ensued between Professor Mortimer and Sally Moulin, during which she purported to be relaying messages from the deceased actor.

I heard whispered comments around me from people who appeared to have fallen for the trick. It was tempting to inform them that they were witnessing a piece of fiction, but I decided it would be better to leave them to their own amusement.

I grew uncomfortable in my seat as communication ensued with the spirit of Thomas Hallam, an actor who had been murdered in the theatre by another actor, Charles

Macklin, during a quarrel. Then boredom set in and I felt a spark of resentment toward Mr Sherman for requesting a review of this sorrowful show.

Eventually, Sally Moulin retreated behind the curtain once again. Professor Mortimer gave an aggrandising speech about Miss Shelley's powers, allowing her enough time to return to her chair in the booth. When he eventually pulled the curtain back, she was slumped over, as though she had been sitting there the entire time. Applause broke out around me, but I struggled to join in, even half-heartedly.

The auditorium fell quiet again as Professor Mortimer untied the ribbons that had bound Miss Shelley to the chair. The ribbon around her wrists must have been tied in such a way that she could slip her hands in and out easily.

The doors to the upper circle swung open behind me, then a voice called out: "Fraud!"

Gasps and mutterings filled the theatre as we turned to see who had interrupted the performance. I was sitting about four rows from the back, so I had a good view of the woman standing there.

"Fraud!" she shouted again. "Every one of you here has paid good money to be lied to!"

CHAPTER 2

N o sooner had the protestor finished her sentence than two men seized her and pulled her out through the door. Immediately sensing she was someone I should speak to, I leapt up from my seat and squeezed my way along the row of knees to get out.

I heard loud protestations in the foyer as I descended the main staircase, and I was just in time to see the woman being pushed out onto the street.

One of the men who had bundled her out – a tall gentleman in a dark suit and waistcoat – scowled at me. "You're not one of *them*, are you?" he asked.

"No, I just need to get some air," I responded, dashing toward the cloakroom to fetch my overcoat.

The October chill felt as refreshing as a splash of cold water on my face. The protesting woman stood a few yards away, still straightening her clothing and recovering her breath.

I stepped over to her. "That was extremely admirable of you," I said.

"Thank you." She was about thirty years old, with wide, stern eyes, a sharp nose and prominent teeth. Her attire was similar to mine, comprising a woollen overcoat, a hat, a scarf and buttoned boots.

"Have you done that sort of thing before?"

"Yes, lots of times. I carry leaflets, too." She unbuttoned her coat and drew a leaflet out from the waistband of her skirt. "I tell people the truth about these charlatans," she added.

I took a leaflet from her. 'All Mediums are Fraudulent' stated the bold title. I read the text beneath, which claimed that spiritualism existed only in the mind, and that science had failed to prove its existence.

"People need to understand what's really happening during these performances," she said. "They're parting with good money to watch someone who is merely pretending to communicate with the spirits."

"I agree," I replied. "I'm only here because someone asked me to be." I explained who I was and the circumstances of my visit.

The woman smiled, seemingly pleased to have met a kindred spirit. "I'm Mrs Bunton," she replied. "Jane Bunton. It's a pleasure to meet you, Mrs Blakely."

"Please call me Penny. Do you have time to talk a little more? I should like to include your views in my article."

"Of course. I'd be delighted to."

"Let's find somewhere a little warmer." I swiftly considered which of the local eateries nearby would be best. "I know an agreeable restaurant close by."

The restaurant I had chosen was Evans's Supper Rooms; a small place close to Covent Garden Piazza. I had eaten there several times before with my husband, James. It was even busier than usual, the throng of bodies creating a warmth that caused my spectacles to steam up as soon as I stepped inside. I wiped them with my scarf as the waiter led us over to a table in the corner.

Once we had placed our order, I asked Jane why she was so keen to expose mediums as frauds.

"My older sister, Lydia, died when I was eight years old. My mother and father were devastated, as were my younger sister, Caroline, and I. Mother was never the same after that – she mourned her greatly. About a year after Lydia's death, my mother had a conversation with a friend who had been to a seance, and who encouraged her to consult a medium and make contact with Lydia." Jane shook her head disapprovingly. "I'll never forget that evening. The medium called at our home in Dulwich Village. She called herself Mrs Romano, though I'm quite certain that wasn't her real name. Mother insisted on all of us attending the seance, but I didn't want to. I was nine years old by this time, and I didn't like Mrs Romano with her eyes ringed in dark pencil and her strange, gaudy garments. She tried to pass herself off as someone from an exotic land, but looking back she was probably just plain old Mrs Brown, born and bred in Battersea.

"We were invited to sit around the table in our parlour in the dark, the only light coming from the embers of the fire. After a few minutes she began to make a strange groaning noise, then she slumped down in her chair and began talking in a very odd voice. It was frightening! Over the course of the next twenty minutes or so, we supposedly heard from Lydia, who told us she was happy, and that she wanted her sisters to work hard at their lessons and look after their mother. I remember being completely transfixed because I thought it was real." She pulled out a handkerchief and wiped her eyes. "I thought it was her. And so did my mother."

I felt a twinge of anger toward Mrs Romano for the false hope she had given the Bunton family.

"And then she came back to her supposedly normal self and told us how exhausting the experience had been for her. I still recall the melodrama of her performance, and looking back I realise how foolish it was. But as a young girl I was taken in, as were my parents in their grief. My mother was overjoyed; she was weeping and laughing. I'd never seen her in such an emotional state. My father probably would have wept, too, if he'd had less restraint. It was only when I grew older that I realised Mrs Romano had been acting deceitfully."

"How did you come to that conclusion?"

"It just stood to reason! I realised there was no evidence that Mrs Romano possessed the skills she claimed to have. She imparted nothing that suggested she had been speaking to our sister. She divulged no personal information about Lydia because Mrs Romano had never met her. All she did was repeat the few facts my parents had shared with her before the seance began. I felt so angry when I realised."

"I'm not surprised."

"I was sixteen when my mother died, and to her very last day she believed Mrs Romano had really communicated with the spirit of her daughter."

"Did your father believe it?"

"He did, although he realises now that Mrs Romano was a fraud. He maintains that she took advantage of our family's weakened, grief-stricken state. I tried to find her years later, but she must have changed her name."

"Why did you want to find her?"

"To challenge her! I wanted her to apologise for fooling us as she did. But I never managed to track her down."

"Is that why you confront other mediums?"

"Yes. Mediums, spiritualists... whichever name they choose for their fraud. I tell everyone the truth."

I admired her determination, but for the purposes of my

article I wondered how she would respond if I challenged her a little. "People pay good money to see magicians," I said. "Why is a medium or spiritualist any different? Isn't it all just a performance?"

"A magician isn't pretending to be someone he isn't. The audience knows his performance is illusion and trickery, and they marvel at his ability to pretend that he's performing magic. Everyone knows his skills include sleight of hand and misdirection. Mediums pretend to have a skill they do not possess. And fooling people into believing they can communicate with spirits while they're in mourning is distressing. The dead should be left in peace, and those who mourn them should be allowed to do so without being given false belief."

"Elizabeth Shelley claimed to be communicating with Joseph Grimaldi and Charles Macklin," I replied. "Surely that wouldn't be terribly upsetting for the audience?"

"Perhaps not, but I still consider it a fraud. And Miss Shelley also conducts private seances, just as Mrs Romano did. These performers are making money under false pretences, and I think it's high time the public understood that."

"People have been challenging spiritualists for several years now. Surely people should be free to make up their own minds on what they choose to believe?"

"Yes, they have a choice, but many accept what happens during these performances without question. I'm extremely angry that these charlatans are allowed to continue practising their deception. It infuriates me."

"Understandably."

"I'm in the process of writing a book that explains how mediums perform their tricks, and I've found a publisher who seems quite interested. Perhaps you'd like to receive a copy to review in your newspaper when it's published?"

"I should like that very much."

"I know that I'll need to be careful, though."

"Why?"

"There are people who don't like what I do."

I felt a pang of concern for her. "Have you received threats?"

"Yes, quite a number." She glanced around her, as if to prevent anyone from overhearing, then turned back to me, her voice a little lower. "I won't let them stop me, though. I refuse to be silenced."

CHAPTER 3

"**M**rs Bunton sounds extremely dedicated to her cause," commented James after I had told him about my evening.

We were seated in the living room of our home in St John's Wood, and Tiger was asleep on my lap.

"I'd say there were worthier causes, though," he continued. "Why waste so much time trying to expose mediums? I thought everybody knew it was all make-believe."

"Not necessarily. Many people believe in it. And she's still upset that her mother was fooled. Vengeance is what motivates her work."

"I can see that. Are you all right, Penny? You look tired."

It was an astute observation. "I feel exhausted," I replied.

"Perhaps you're doing too much."

"Nonsense! All I've done today is work at my typewriter and attend the show."

"And stay out late with your new friend." He yawned and checked his watch. "Time for us both to retire, I think." He got to his feet. "Have you opened the letter that arrived for you this morning?"

"No, I didn't see it."

"Mrs Oliver must have tidied it away somewhere. She's got into the habit of doing that recently. Do you remember that letter I received from the bank? I didn't lay eyes on it for three days!"

I sat and stroked Tiger's soft fur while he went off to find the letter. She blinked her eyes open and purred.

"Here it is," James said when he returned a moment later. "It looks like your father's handwriting to me."

"Father?" I took the letter from him. I hadn't seen my father since he had travelled to Liverpool to meet his common-law wife and children, who had just arrived from Colombia. My father, a former plant-hunter, had been lost in South America for ten years, and had, during that time, fallen in love with an Amazonian woman.

Dearest Penny and James

I hope this letter finds you both fit and well. I can scarcely believe that it is almost eight weeks since I arrived here in Liverpool. What a welcoming and hospitable city it is! The Liverpudlians have more than demonstrated their ability to accommodate the needs of travellers from the world over; accustomed, as they are, to meeting the contrary needs of foreigners. Not that I count myself one! However, as a gentleman who has travelled a great deal, I occasionally feel like a stranger in my own land.

My dear wife and children are foreigners indeed. It has been most delightful making their acquaintance once again, and I am very much looking forward to you and your sister visiting us here. We are renting a most agreeable house on a pleasant thoroughfare. There is plenty of room for us all – more than I ever could have hoped to afford in London. Such a costly city! One of the costliest in the world, I shouldn't wonder.

You would likely expect heads to turn as I take an afternoon stroll with my family, the members of which are distinctly foreign in appearance. But I am pleased to report that very few people stare at us. Perhaps the Liverpudlians are so accustomed to visitors of all creeds and colours that they have no peculiar interest in anyone from foreign climes.

It's safe to say that we have well and truly made the city our home. This was not my original plan, as you know. It had always been my intention to live in London with my new family, but I need not repeat to you the struggle I faced in finding somewhere affordable for us to live. We have discovered a delightful little school for the children to attend, and they have already learned a good number of English words. I'm so very proud of them!

They were rather perplexed at first by the size and scale of the city, and by the noise and smells. I admit that I was concerned about them when they first arrived, but they have adapted remarkably quickly. I took them to a sweet shop and the delight on their faces as they sucked boiled sweets for the first time was a joy to behold!

It truly is a wonder, and I think you can probably infer from the tone of my letter, Penny, that we are having a simply wonderful time. We have enjoyed trips to the zoo and the fairground, and the children are particularly fascinated by the large ships and cranes in the dockyard. Now that the weather has turned, I doubt there will be too many excursions for a while. I worry about their constitutions as winter befalls us, given that they are quite unused to European winters and their chills, but I shall ensure that they are kept warm.

I could write far more, Penny, but I should like to catch the post in time. Dear Eliza has informed me that she has booked your train tickets for the 31st of October. I can't tell you how much I'm looking forward to seeing you. Having all my family together in one place will be a dream come true! I am eagerly counting down the days.

With very fondest regards,
Your Father

"Eliza has booked tickets!" I exclaimed. "That was rather presumptuous of her."

"For which date?"

"The 31st of October."

"That's about four weeks away. It'll be nice to finally meet your father's family."

"I don't know about that." Despite having known about them for several months, I was still coming to terms with the fact that I had a number of half-brothers and sisters.

"I'm sure that seeing them will help, Penny."

"Perhaps it will." I felt my jaw clench. Much as I had tried to forgive my father for remaining silent during his ten-year absence, it was still a struggle to feel completely at ease about it.

CHAPTER 4

The familiar roar of the printing presses greeted me as I stepped into the offices of the *Morning Express* newspaper on Fleet Street the following day. Having spent the morning writing my article on Elizabeth Shelley and Jane Bunton, I was ready to hand it over to the editor, Mr Sherman.

I had been working as a reporter on the newspaper for ten years when the proprietor asked me to leave prior to my marriage. Thankfully, Mr Sherman still commissioned me to write the occasional article, and I felt happy not to have left my former work altogether.

The roar from the presses in the basement faded a little as I climbed the staircase to the newsroom. I made my way along the narrow corridor and was about to push open the door when I heard raised voices coming from Mr Sherman's office. I wondered if one of the compositors was in trouble, as usual.

"How lovely it is to see your face again, Miss Green," said my former colleague, Edgar Fish.

"*Mrs Blakely*," corrected Frederick Potter.

"Oh, that's right. Apologies, Mrs Blakely. Just force of habit, I'm afraid. How's your schoolboy inspector?"

"He's very well," I replied, smiling at the nickname Edgar had always used for James. "Although his schoolboy days are long behind him now."

"Same for all of us, I suppose. How I miss those days."

"I feel sorry for whoever that is in Mr Sherman's office," I said. "He appears to be receiving quite the telling off."

Edgar grimaced. "Mr Conway's in there."

"Mr Conway?" I struggled to believe that voices would be raised in such a manner while the proprietor of the *Morning Express* was present.

Edgar and Frederick exchanged glances.

Then Edgar turned to me, lowering his voice. "In truth, Mrs Blakely, it's been rather troublesome here recently. Mr Sherman and Mr Conway haven't been seeing eye to eye."

"I'm sorry to hear it. Both are known for their strong opinions, I suppose. Perhaps it's to be expected now and again."

"Yes, they both have strong opinions, but there appears to be something a little more persistent in their disagreements these days." He lowered his voice even more. "People are saying the drink has finally got to him."

"To whom?"

"Mr Conway. He's always enjoyed a drink, but these days he enjoys it a little too much."

"Or perhaps he doesn't enjoy it at all," added Frederick. "He seems thoroughly miserable."

"That's probably on account of his wife engaging in an affair with the editor of *The Holborn Gazette*," added Edgar.

"*What?*" I felt my jaw hang open for a moment, then swiftly resumed a more ladylike expression. *The Holborn Gazette* was the principal rival of the *Morning Express*. "But that's unthinkable!" I continued. "An affair is one thing, but an affair with an arch-enemy is quite another."

Edgar shook his head. "One might have a little sympathy with Mr Conway if he wasn't such a..."

His words hung in the air as we each silently finished the sentence with our own insults. We had all been on the receiving end of his sharp tongue in the past. I held little affection for the proprietor given that he had insisted on me leaving my job just before I married.

"I suppose I feel a little sorry for him," conceded Frederick.

"Perhaps." Edgar nodded. "However, Mrs Conway's dalliance is beginning to affect the mood in the newsroom. Mr Sherman is having to endure a great deal of interference as he attempts to produce the paper each day. It wouldn't be such a problem if Conway's suggestions made sense, but the effects of the drink mean that they generally don't. One of his recent requests was for an editorial on the unreliability of *The Holborn Gazette* as a source of news. Whether or not one believes that, it's not the sort of thing we should be publishing. He was pursuing a personal vendetta."

"Understandably so," added Frederick.

"Yes, but he can't use the newspaper to wreak his revenge. It's all been such a strain on Mr Sherman's nerves, and..."

Edgar stopped as the newsroom door swung open and the editor strode in. His shirt sleeves were rolled up, and a pipe stuck out from beneath his thick black moustache. Still red in the face from his encounter with Mr Conway, he paused to mop his brow with a crumpled handkerchief.

"Mrs Blakely!" he said. "How was the show?"

"It was most enlightening."

"Elizabeth Shelley's quite something, isn't she? I decided we had to write about her when I saw her in action a couple of weeks ago. I don't know how she does it! I take it you have your article ready for me."

I nodded and handed it to him. He began to read through it.

"I should like to see her myself," said Edgar. "I'm never quite sure whether these people are genuine or not. But if not, how do they do it? Even if they're not who they purport to be, they must be very clever to make it look as if they are."

Mr Sherman scowled. "From a cursory glance at this, Mrs Blakely, I can see that you've included a comment from someone else in the article. Who is this Mrs Bunton?"

"She interrupted the show, sir. She believes that spiritualism is fraudulent, and she wanted to inform the audience of her opinion."

"But why have you included her claims in the article? It was supposed to be about Elizabeth Shelley."

"I realise that, and I began my work with the full intention of focusing solely on Miss Shelley. But I had quite a long discussion with Mrs Bunton, and I thought it would be of interest to our readers to hear both sides of the story."

"Both sides? This is supposed to be an article about spiritualism and Miss Shelley's unique powers."

"Are they truly powers, though, sir? Or are they little more than clever trickery?"

"I don't like to believe that it's trickery myself, I think it's a gift. You're always going to get the naysayers, but this article isn't for them. It's for the people who want to read about Miss Shelley's powers." He thrust the piece of paper back at me. "If I'd asked you for a discourse on the merits of spiritualism, this would have done just fine. But that is *not* what I asked for, Mrs Blakely. Would you kindly rewrite it please?" He turned on his heel and strode out of the newsroom, leaving the door to slam behind him.

Silence ensued, and I felt a prickle of shame in my face. I was unaccustomed to the editor rejecting my work.

"Oh dear, Mrs Blakely. I don't think he's very happy, is he?" said Edgar. "Don't take it to heart. He's only in a foul mood because Conway's upset him again."

It was disappointing that I had to write an article that conveyed the merits of spiritualism without any sense of balance. "This serves to remind me why I left the newspaper in the first place," I said.

"You left the newspaper because you got married, Mrs Blakely."

"You're right, Edgar, but I can't say that I've missed it. I think that's due to my being able to write whatever I want these days. Being told how to compose my articles doesn't sit well with me, especially when it fails to align with my personal beliefs."

"Don't tell me you think Miss Shelley is a fraud!" said Edgar.

"I'm afraid so. I simply cannot understand how anyone is taken in by it."

"Do you really not believe any of it, Mrs Blakely?"

"I'm afraid not, Edgar."

He shook his head. "Well, where's the fun in that? It's good to have just a little belief in these things. I like to think there must be some sort of magic in this world."

"I like to think that too, Edgar, but I didn't find anything magical about Miss Shelley."

I sighed, wondering how I would bring myself to write anything vaguely flattering about her.

CHAPTER 5

I dined that evening with my sister, Eliza, at the Fitzroy Dining Rooms; a smart place with gleaming white table-cloths and an elaborately corniced ceiling. Voices hummed around us, cutlery chinked and the smell of roasted meat made my stomach grumble as we waited for our food to arrive.

"I didn't know you had booked the train tickets for our trip to see Father and his family," I said.

"Oh yes, I was going to tell you about that this evening. How did you find out?"

"He told me in a letter."

"Ah, he got to you before I did."

"I hadn't realised you were planning the trip."

"I thought we had agreed that we would visit him."

"Yes, but we hadn't agreed *when*."

"I just thought I'd get on with it because it seemed to be taking a long while to decide."

"But how did you know that the dates you chose would be suitable?"

"Are they not?"

"I don't know yet."

"What else do you have planned?"

"Writing, reporting... My *work*, Ellie." Ever since my marriage to James, my sister seemed to assume I did nothing at all with my time.

"Are you busy working on another of your cases, Penelope?" This question was delivered with a tone of disapproval.

"Not a case, as such, but I do have work to do."

"What are you writing about at the moment?"

"Spiritualism."

"Really?" Her eyes widened. "That subject interests me greatly. I know it sounds like a foolish notion, but I truly believe that some people can contact the spirits of the dead."

"Surely not?"

"There was that friend of Mother's back home in Derbyshire. Do you remember her? Mrs Gilligan, her name was. She had a gift. She would regularly gather the ladies together at her home and communicate with the spirits of their dead family members."

"Or so she claimed."

"She was very convincing, by all accounts."

"Mrs Gilligan presumably had quite a good knowledge of her friends' loved ones," I ventured. "In which case, it wouldn't have been too tricky to construct a message from their dearly departed."

"I think it's quite possible that some people are in possession of a sixth sense. And why shouldn't the spirits of the dead attempt to contact us? Some people depart this life so suddenly that many things are left undone and unsaid. It makes enormous sense that they would try to get in touch in order to convey such messages."

"I cannot agree, Ellie," I responded. "Even if that were the case, I've never come across a medium who is able to relay such messages. They merely communicate the information they have guessed at themselves."

"You seem determined to disbelieve, Penelope."

"I am."

"I can see that your work on spiritualism is to contain an element of bias. I'm not a journalist, but even I know that you should approach such topics with an open mind, at the very least."

I took a sip of water to prevent myself from snapping in response.

"Meanwhile, my own work has been occupying my time enormously," she continued. "I'm monitoring several tenants now, one of whom worries me a great deal."

Eliza worked for a philanthropist named Susan Barrington, who provided homes for people living in poverty. The properties were offered at a low rent, and the tenants received practical assistance from a team of employees to which my sister belonged.

"This particular tenant is a widow with six children," she said, "the youngest of whom is in a weakened state due to an illness of some sort. The little mite soldiers on as best she might, but she has become so weak that she can barely stand."

"That's very sad to hear."

"It's sad to witness, too. The mother, Mrs Reddings, has to go out to work in a soap factory, as do the eldest siblings, a boy and a girl. It's left to the next boy, aged just eight years old, to mind his younger brothers and sisters – including the weakling – with some help from the seven-year-old. Miss Barrington provides excellent accommodation, but it isn't particularly spacious. This family of seven occupies just two rooms. Poor Mrs Reddings is so tired and exhausted with worry." Eliza paused and shook her head, and there was dampness in her eyes. "I just wish there were something more I could do."

"You're already helping them as best you can."

"But it isn't enough! They have a roof over their heads and they're just about able to feed themselves on a very basic diet, but it isn't a diet I would wish my own children to have. All the family needs is a sum of money to help them get back on their feet, and I'm in an excellent position to help."

"Really?"

"I think ten pounds would do it."

"That's a significant sum of money, Ellie." I estimated it would take a street seller or shop worker three months to earn that much. "Can you be sure that the money would help them make a significant change to their lives?"

"Of course it would. How could it not? Mrs Reddings would be able to buy new boots and clothes for her children, and she'd be able to afford to feed them properly."

"And when the money runs out?"

Eliza fixed me with her brown eyes. "You think I shouldn't help them, Penelope?"

"I didn't say that. I'm just wondering what would happen once the money had been spent."

She shrugged. "The family would make it last a long time, and they'd have a better standard of living by then. Perhaps Mrs Reddings could stop work for a little while, and then the children could concentrate on their education."

"It sounds as if it might help them for a short while, Ellie."

"A short while? I'm hoping it would cover their expenses for at least a year, possibly longer. During that time, Mrs Reddings could learn how to manage her money more effectively. That's a common problem with the working classes, you see. They don't always know how to manage their money properly when they have it. I suppose I should be grateful there's no Mr Reddings to spend it all on beer after a hard day's work. Some families get themselves into a dreadful state, Penny. I often see money lenders loitering outside the factory gates on a Friday evening, waiting for the men to hand over their pay packets in repayment of the loans they've previously taken out. I try to educate all my tenants on the matter of looking after their money. And if I'm able to gift them something as well, that's what I feel I should do."

"Isn't there a risk that it would ruin the relationship between you and Mrs Reddings?"

"How so?"

"She may feel indebted to you, and that could make a delicate situation like this rather awkward. At the present time, your role in helping her is clearly defined. If you alter it by becoming personally involved—"

"You don't have to see them suffer, Penelope. I do!"

I knew there was no use in suggesting the idea was unwise. Eliza could match me for stubbornness.

"If I choose to help, it's crucial that Miss Barrington never finds out," she continued. "Giving money directly to tenants is frowned upon, and she's already given us a lecture on the subject, but I just can't help myself. Whenever I visit that family and see the abject poverty they're living in, I desperately want to do something to help.

"How can I keep all my money to myself when I see such need? I can't donate on a regular basis, as I don't know what my own circumstances will be in the future. I have some money left over from the divorce, but that'll run out before long. I'll give what I know I can manage in the meantime, and I'm sure that will be of some help."

I resigned myself to the fact that her mind was made up. "You know your tenants and their circumstances far better than I do, Ellie. It's for you to decide whether you're able to help them or not." I quickly changed the subject. "How's Francis?"

Eliza and our librarian friend Francis Edwards had been courting since his return from finding our father in Amazonia earlier in the year.

She smiled. "We enjoy a pleasant walk together every Sunday afternoon, come rain or shine. He also visits me at home on a Wednesday evening and we play cards. I enjoy his company immensely."

"That's good to hear."

"I'm beginning to wonder whether our relationship will ever progress, however."

"You want him to propose?"

"I should like to know whether or not he intends to. If he could give me some indication one way or the other, I shall know where my life is heading. Each week is much the same as the previous, and I don't know how well that bodes for our future."

"Why don't you ask him about his plans?"

She laughed. "I couldn't do that, Penelope! How terribly impolite. What would he think of me?"

"He knows you well, and I'm sure he wouldn't pass judgement on you for asking. If you feel uncertain about the future, you should ask him what his views are. You needn't ask so directly; merely bring the matter up in conversation. That's what I would do."

Eliza's lips thinned when I made this last comment. "I can't help but think back," she commented.

"What do you mean?"

"Do you remember when Francis was keen on courting you?"

"Oh, Ellie, I don't think there's any need to discuss that now. A lot has happened since then." I felt heat in my face as I recalled him making protestations of love while we were travelling together in a hackney carriage one evening. James had been engaged to marry another woman at the time.

"Do you ever think back to the time when he was ready to propose to you?" she said.

I shifted in my chair, distinctly uncomfortable about the topic of conversation. "Ellie, I don't want to think about that. We all know it would have been a big mistake. I'm married to James, and you and Francis should follow suit. We won't help ourselves by thinking about the past."

CHAPTER 6

"You're scowling, Penny," said James at breakfast. "This doesn't signify a good start to the day."

"Scowling?" I attempted to smooth my brow and took a sip of tea.

"Something's bothering you."

"Yes, it is." I had been dwelling on my visit to the *Morning Express* offices the previous day. "I can't believe Mr Sherman wants me to rewrite the article and make it more sympathetic to the spiritualist. I think the story people will be most interested in is that of the woman challenging the spiritualist's claims. I can't believe many people these days believe a woman like Miss Shelley has genuine powers."

"Perhaps Mr Sherman is a believer."

"I'm wondering if he is. He didn't like the idea of me including Mrs Bunton's claims at all, but I don't want to write the article if I can't include anyone else's views."

James broke the shell of his boiled egg with a spoon. "Perhaps there's no need for you to waste any more of your time on it," he responded.

"Waste my time? It's my job, James! I just feel so frustrated when people try to tell me how to write my articles."

He peeled several pieces of eggshell off and rested them on his saucer. "I know you enjoy your work, Penny, but you're not obliged to write for Mr Sherman any more. You have a choice. I really can't see how it's worth your while lamenting over an article he wanted you to write when there was no need for you to do it in the first place."

I felt a snap of anger. "Are you belittling my work?"

He sat back in his chair, surprised by my response. "Of course not. You know I have great respect for everything you do, and have done, over the years. You're incredibly good at it, Penny. But if something's bothering you, you have the choice to walk away and work on something more palatable instead."

It was true that I could more or less choose what I wanted to work on these days, but I had never walked away from a piece of work before. Doing so felt like a betrayal of my core principles.

James pulled his notebook out of his jacket pocket and began leafing through it as he ate his egg.

"How's the jewel thief case progressing?" I asked.

"Poorly." He turned several more pages impatiently. "We thought we knew who was behind the robberies, but we've been proven wrong. There aren't many people who possess the variety of skills this gang has. I'm wondering whether it's a gang of foreigners, actually."

James had seemed particularly distracted of late. I'd attempted to be sympathetic; familiar, as I was with the demands of a thought-consuming investigation. However, I had found his manner dismissive at times, as if he considered his work to be more important than mine.

He finished his egg, then gave me a thoughtful glance, as

though he were aware of the sliver of resentment I was harbouring.

"You're still scowling," he commented.

"So are you."

"That's because more than fifty thousand pounds' worth of jewellery has gone missing from Hatton Garden jewellery shops over the past month and we don't have a clue who's behind the thefts."

"Therefore you have a valid reason to scowl and I don't?"

"I didn't say that, Penny."

"You implied it, though."

"No, I didn't!"

"It's all right for you to be frustrated about your work, but not me. Is that it?"

"Now that's simply not true."

"I know, but you make me feel as if it is."

"I'm sorry if that's the case. It wasn't my intention." He sighed and sat back in his chair. "Penny, I'm rather busy at the moment, and although I'm sorry to hear that you're frustrated about your article, it isn't the be-all and end-all. You can just turn your hand to something more interesting. I can't see the appeal of writing about spiritualists, anyway. They're just putting on an act like any other performer. If people want to believe it, that's up to them. But I don't see how you're undertaking any great moral service by presenting both sides of the argument in an article. I think most people's minds will already be made up one way or the other. Some are foolish enough to still believe it, but I imagine most people don't really care."

"And you are one of the latter."

"You're right. I don't care about spiritualism. It rarely entertains my thoughts. What I *do* care about is solving this case."

I travelled to the reading room at the British Library with a sour taste in my mouth. I never enjoyed arguing with James, but neither did I like to feel that my work was less important than his. Perhaps I was fortunate to have a profession at all. The limited number of women who were able to pursue a career largely had to relinquish it when they married. I knew that my position was an unusual one, and perhaps it was only natural that it should feel difficult at times.

I stepped off the omnibus at Great Russell Street. The colonnaded facade of the British Museum to my left was indistinct in the fog. Across the road to my right sat the Museum Tavern, where James and I had conducted our first proper conversation two years ago. I still clearly recalled the grey woollen suit he had worn that day and the blue tie that had matched his eyes. He had sipped at his tankard of brown stout and done his best to persuade me to help him solve the Lizzie Dixie murder case. I had sipped at my sherry and felt all resistance slipping as my interest in the handsome young detective grew.

And now we were so accustomed to each other that we readily argued, taking each other's presence for granted. *Was this how our marriage was supposed to be?* The thought created an uncomfortable lump in my throat.

"Penny!" Francis greeted me with a loud whisper and a wide grin when I entered the reading room. "How are you?"

The warmth of his welcome tempted me to share my troubled thoughts with him, but the quiet of the library was not a suitable place to do so.

"Very well, thank you," I responded.

"Wonderful." He pushed a lock of sandy hair away from his spectacles. "Are you looking for anything in particular today?"

"I should like to look at a book that Professor Joseph Mortimer published on his investigations into spiritualism."

"Interesting. Is this a new interest of yours, Penny?"

"Oh, no. It's just some research for an article I'm working on. I'm interested in finding out how Professor Mortimer qualifies his belief in mediums and spiritualism. Personally, I think it's all a great fraud."

"It's one of those subjects that divides opinion, isn't it? Much like a belief in ghosts. I'm surprised at how many people hold to such beliefs in this age of modern science. However, I also think there are plenty of rational people who, in the cold light of day, have no belief in the supernatural at all, but may, in the dead of night, experience something they cannot fully explain. In those circumstances, they may reluctantly accept a supernatural explanation. Have I ever told you that I once encountered a ghost?"

This admission surprised me. "No! You actually saw one?"

"Not quite, and I really don't believe in them, but something happened once that I simply cannot explain. I was staying at an old fifteenth-century inn in York and was just dozing off when I heard heavy footsteps in the corridor beyond my door. I thought it rather inconsiderate that someone should make no effort to quieten the noise of their boots at such a late hour. However, I allowed it to pass and drifted off. A short while later the footsteps returned, and this time they paced up and down the corridor. At this point I decided to have a word with the fellow who was so intent on disturbing my slumber. I got out of bed, lit my lantern and made my way over to the door. I unlocked it, opened it and... guess what? There was no one there."

I felt a shiver run down my spine. "Might the man just have gone into his room?"

"If he did, I heard no sound of any door or lock. That long, dark corridor was completely silent. And I'll tell you something else: the temperature had dropped so low that I could see my clouded breath in the air."

"Really?" I considered Francis a rational person and not someone who was prone to telling tales.

"Yes, it was absolutely freezing. I was rather perturbed, as you might imagine. I returned to bed, but I couldn't sleep. Instead, I just lay there, wide awake. Perhaps I drifted off eventually, I can't be sure. But much later that night the foot-steps returned."

"Oh, no!"

"I dared not get out of bed that time; I couldn't bring myself to do it. So I simply lay there without sleeping a wink."

"Did you speak to anyone about it the following morning?"

"Oh, yes. I discussed it with the hotel manager, who told me other guests had reported hearing the same thing. I was relieved to hear that I hadn't been the only one, but it was still perturbing that it had happened. The manager also related an interesting story to me. The Battle of Marston Moor had been fought near the inn in 1644, at the Siege of York during the English Civil War. The building was inhabited by important Royalist commanders during the siege. Is your Civil War knowledge extensive?"

"No."

"Very well. The Royalists – the ones who supported the king – lost the battle, and York eventually had to surrender to the Parliamentarians. One of the Royalist commanders, I forget his name now, was seen returning to the inn shortly after the battle. Many witnesses confirmed it, yet they were surprised to see him, as all his comrades had either been killed or captured. It was said that he paced the upper corridor of the inn dejectedly and refused all food, drink and conversation. Then, all of a sudden, he was seen no more. A few days later, it was learned that he had, in fact, been killed during the battle and couldn't possibly have returned to the inn."

"In which case, they had seen his ghost?"

"Supposedly so. A rather silly story, isn't it? It's the type of tale I would normally dismiss, but it was difficult to do so having encountered those unearthly footsteps."

"And you only heard the story the following morning?"

"Exactly. I struggle to believe it was really a ghost, but I honestly don't know what else to think."

"Intriguing, to say the least," said a thick-whiskered man who was working at a desk close by. "And while I appreciate the brief interlude to the drudgery of my work, might it be possible to have a little quiet, please?"

"Of course." Francis's face reddened. "I apologise for the interruption."

Once Francis had helped me locate Professor Mortimer's book, I spent several hours perusing the experiments described within it. Many were accompanied by informative diagrams which showed how the various apparatuses had been set up. Professor Mortimer had conducted his experiments with Miss Shelley in the basement of his home and had asked colleagues to join him as independent observers. Objects had been observed to move and levitate of their own accord, and Miss Shelley had appeared to play notes on an accordion without actually touching it.

After making notes for a while, I sat back in my chair and pondered the veracity of these experiments. I still struggled to believe that Miss Shelley possessed any special powers, but she did seem to possess an unusual ability of some sort. Perhaps it was little more than the ability to convince others of her trickery. *Did Professor Mortimer genuinely believe she had a gift?* I wondered if she might have conducted some sort of hypnosis on him. I had read a little about the practice but didn't fully understand how it worked.

When I finished reading through Professor Mortimer's experiments, I decided he had convinced himself of Miss Shelley's powers. And it seemed he had embarked on his studies with a desire to do so. There was little evidence of any impartial application of science in his experiments.

I closed the book and carried it back to its shelf. It was a piece of work that appeared to combine fact and fiction. *But where did the boundary between the two lie?* I had previously thought the dividing line was perfectly clear, but having heard Francis's story about the sinister footsteps, I had begun to doubt my own views.

CHAPTER 7

James was late home that evening. I seated myself in the living room with my notebook on my lap and Tiger beside me on the settee. I intended to draft article ideas, but my glance kept wandering over to the clock on the mantelpiece.

"Would you like to eat now, Mrs Blakely? Or will you wait until Mr Blakely has returned?" The housekeeper, Mrs Oliver, stood in the doorway, wiping her hands on her apron.

"I'd like to wait until he returns," I responded. "It'll stay warm on the sideboard, Mrs Oliver, so there's no need for you to wait."

She glanced at the clock. "Well, I'm happy to stay until eight, but after that I'll need to get off."

I thanked her, and she left the room. I wondered if Mrs Oliver had overheard our argument at breakfast. *Was that why James wasn't yet home? Perhaps he had joined his colleagues for a drink after work, preferring their company to that of his grumpy wife at home?*

I ran through our exchange at breakfast in my mind and tried to recall my exact words, wondering which had upset him the most. It hadn't been our most unpleasant argument, but it had left me feeling quite disgruntled, and I imagined James would be feeling the same way.

I reread the ideas I had scribbled down and struck a line through most of them. It was impossible to concentrate on anything until I had spoken to James again. I felt a need to clear the air between us. I pushed my notebook to one side, leaned back and closed my eyes, hoping to doze until James returned.

A knock at the door startled me. I knew it couldn't be James because he had a key. *Had he forgotten it? Might it be someone bearing bad news?*

Mrs Oliver answered the door, then entered the room with an envelope in her hand. "A telegram for you, Mrs Blakely."

I tore it open and was relieved to see that it came from James. He gave a reason for his detention, and it wasn't a happy one.

"Is everything all right?" asked the housekeeper.

"Jane Bunton's been murdered." I stared at the brief message in my hand, which included an address in Highgate. The telegram gave me an opportunity to be one of the first reporters on the scene.

"Jane Bunton?"

"A woman I met a few days ago."

"Murdered, you say? How awful!"

"I've got to get there," I said.

"But it's dark, foggy and cold out there now, Mrs Blakely."

"Never mind." I dashed upstairs to fetch my hat, scarf and overcoat.

I hailed a cab on Finchley Road and didn't envy the horse having to make the steady ascent up to Hampstead and High-gate. I huddled into the seat and pulled my scarf up to my chin. Outside, gas lights glimmered faintly in the fog and people were reduced to little more than passing shadows.

Who could have harmed Jane Bunton? I thought about the determined young woman and how I had admired her sense of purpose. *Interrupting performances would inevitably anger people, but who could have been angered enough to actually murder her?* I had barely known the woman, and yet I felt a heavy sadness for her loss.

After leaving Hampstead, the cab crossed the heath on Spaniards Road. The lamps on the cab illuminated little more than the horse's hindquarters, and its hooves struck a lonely sound on the road. This had once been a stretch of road frequented by highwaymen. I glanced into the darkness around me and Francis's ghost story came to mind. I didn't want to believe any of it, but he had seemed quite convinced of what he'd heard. I felt a prickle at the back of my neck and tried to push the story out of my mind. Although I had never felt I was in any danger on my journey, my discomfort eased when the dim lights of the Spaniards Inn emerged from the fog.

Five minutes later, the cab pulled up on Hampstead Lane in Highgate. From what I could see in the fog, we were in a respectable, tree-lined street containing spacious, modern houses. Ahead of me, a cluster of shadowy figures holding torchlights had gathered at a gateway. Beyond the gate, a flight of steps led up to the door of a tall house. I paid the driver, climbed out and found a police constable. I introduced myself as Detective Inspector James Blakely's wife.

"Please stay here," he said. "You don't want to get any closer to the house, it's not a pretty sight. I'll fetch your husband."

A few moments later, I was reunited with James. The upset of our disagreement and the death of Jane Bunton overwhelmed me for a moment, and I threw my arms around him. His woollen overcoat was damp from the fog.

Aware that his colleagues were around us, I quickly pulled away. "What's happened?" I asked.

"Mrs Bunton was found dead on her doorstep." He gestured at the house behind him. "Someone called at her home and asked for her in person. Then she was shot."

My blood ran cold. "That's awful. I can't understand it. Were any other people at home?"

"Yes, her husband, Samuel Bunton. He's extremely distressed, as you can imagine. He was the one who answered the door and fetched his wife when the caller asked for her."

"And who was the caller?"

"A young woman in a cape, but she didn't stay. By the time Mrs Bunton came to the door, the young woman had fled down the steps. It was someone else who fired the shot. He was standing in the gateway."

"Two people were involved? Did Mr Bunton see the man who fired the shot?"

"Not particularly well, as the fog hampered his view. He told me he saw the silhouette of a man wearing a hat and an overcoat, but that was all. He couldn't tell me his age or anything more about his appearance. Mr Bunton immediately gave chase. There was no sign of the young woman, and the man ran down that way towards the centre of Highgate." He pointed down the street. "Mr Bunton soon lost sight of him in the fog, but we've found a witness who saw a man running along The Grove, heading toward Highgate Cemetery. It may have been the assailant or it may have been someone else."

James gestured at the neighbouring property. "The neighbour at this house here, Mrs Hargreaves, came out when she heard the gunshot. Mr Bunton called out to her for help, and she looked after Mrs Bunton while he chased after the man who'd shot her. She did her very best to save Mrs Bunton, but sadly it was not to be."

"A young woman called at the house..." I mused. Elizabeth Shelley immediately came to mind. She wouldn't have been happy that Jane Bunton had interrupted her show. "Professor Mortimer," I said. "Perhaps he shot Jane Bunton?"

"We'll be looking into that possibility," replied James, "but there could be others, too. At this stage, I need to gather as much evidence as I can. We've got men searching all the surrounding streets, houses, parkland and the cemetery, too. The pair of them will have got far away from here by now. I've just asked someone to put the word out to cab drivers, as one of them may have picked the attackers up."

A sergeant strode over and asked to speak with James. "I'll leave you to get on with your work," I said.

He smiled and squeezed my hand before departing.

"It's too terrible for words," said a voice from behind me.

I turned to see a tall woman of about forty. Her handsome features were just discernible in the flicker of passing torch-light. She wore a long overcoat and a fur-trimmed hat.

"I did all I could," she continued, "but I don't suppose she stood a chance." Her voice cracked.

"Are you her neighbour?" I queried, assuming I was talking to Mrs Hargreaves.

"Yes. I jumped out of my skin when I heard the gunshot. I can't even explain how loud it was. I've never heard anything like that before. I immediately knew something had to be wrong. I ran out here, and when I saw it was Jane... I just couldn't believe it. Who would want to do that to her? She must have been mistaken for someone else, I suppose. I did what I could..." She shook her head in dismay. "There was an awful lot of blood, and I really hoped I could do something to save her, but she was turning pale so quickly and her eyes were closing. Samuel had run off after the shooter, and I shouted for someone to fetch a doctor. More people had come out of their houses by then. Someone had a coat, which we put over Jane, and we tried to make her more comfortable. That sounds rather foolish when you consider how seriously injured she was."

She fell quiet for a moment, then wiped a handkerchief over her face.

"Did you see her attackers?" I asked.

"No. Samuel told me there were two of them, but I didn't see either."

"This must be extremely upsetting for you," I said.

"Jane was such a delightful woman. I can't understand why anybody would have wanted to harm her. The police absolutely *have* to catch this man! He can't go around shooting people whenever he feels like it."

I offered Mrs Hargreaves my sincere condolences, then called at some of the surrounding homes, introducing myself as a news reporter. My plan was to type a quick report as soon as I returned home, and send it straight to the *Morning Express* offices by messenger so it could be published in the morning.

Some of the neighbours preferred not to speak to me, but others were more talkative. Everyone spoke kindly of Jane Bunton, and their descriptions of her fitted well with the impression I had from our recent meeting. All considered her to have been a thoughtful, intelligent, kind woman. It was difficult to comprehend that this had really happened.

I walked toward The Grove, a neighbouring street, and spoke to the witness who had seen the man running away in the direction of the cemetery.

"The noise of the gun made me look out of the window," she said. Her name was Mrs Rogers. "Then I saw him running past. We're lucky enough to have a gas lamp outside, so I managed to catch a glimpse of him."

"What did he look like?"

"It was difficult to tell. He was wearing a hat and an overcoat – as anyone would on a cold, foggy night."

"Did you happen to notice the colour of his hair?" Professor Mortimer's wavy grey hair and whiskers came to mind.

"I'm afraid not. As I said, he was wearing a hat, and I only glimpsed him for a moment."

"Was he young? Old?"

"I really couldn't tell you, I'm afraid."

Either way, he had been nimble enough to get well away from the scene without delay.

CHAPTER 8

The fog had cleared by the time I walked to Regent's Park the following morning. I planned to head through the park and then take the omnibus, which departed from a road on the eastern edge and would take me to Camden Town.

I wanted to interview Professor Mortimer and Miss Shelley to assess their response to Jane Bunton's murder. To my mind, they were obvious suspects, and I hoped an interview would help me — and the public — decide if they had something to hide.

I had consulted the directory at the post office and found Professor Mortimer's address in Camden Square. The omnibus ride took just fifteen minutes, so I soon found myself on the busy high street.

Camden Town was not a place I had visited often, but I already knew a little of its character. Having begun as a respectable suburb in Georgian times — a rural area between Hampstead, Highgate and London town — it had grown considerably in recent years. The construction of Regents Canal and the railways had prompted a surge in new homes for workers, and streets of terraced houses now stretched in every direction. Their inhabitants were employed in the sprawling goods yards of Euston, St Pancras and King's Cross railway stations, as well as within the industrial sites of Camden Town itself. Gin distillers and wine merchants had established themselves in the area, as had several piano makers, who made regular use of the canal to transport their heavy, cumbersome instruments.

I travelled by horse tram past rows of little shops, over the canal and under a railway bridge toward Camden Square. The houses in this area were modern and spacious, in stark contrast to the cramped houses near the factories and railway lines.

A short walk brought me to Camden Square; a rectangular expanse of green bordered by large, attractive, semi-detached homes. A church spire rose above the russet-leaved trees at the far end of the square.

I soon found Professor Mortimer's home. Three storeys high, it had tall windows, a well-maintained front garden and a flight of steps leading up to a polished front door.

A maid answered, and I introduced myself, adding that I had recently attended one of Miss Shelley's shows. I gave her my card and waited in the hallway, hoping the professor would be willing to speak to me.

A few moments later, I was shown into a front room, which boasted well-polished furniture and a colourful, orna-mental rug. Paintings of classical buildings – one of which I recognised as the Parthenon at Athens – hung on the walls, and several display cabinets contained miniature copies of Renaissance sculptures.

Professor Mortimer stepped into the room, his thick grey hair and whiskers a little more unruly than when I had seen him on stage. He was slighter than I remembered and wore a smart, dark morning suit. He held a book in his hand, which he placed on an occasional table before greeting me. I saw that it was a compilation of Greek tragedies.

He greeted me with a smile. "How nice to meet you, Mrs Blakely. You're a news reporter, is that right?"

If my unannounced visit had bothered him, he was determined not to show it.

"Yes. I write for the *Morning Express*, along with several other publications."

"I sometimes take the *Morning Express*. It's a decent newspaper."

"I like to think so. I hope you don't mind me visiting you this morning, but I happened to be present on the evening that Mrs Jane Bunton interrupted your show, and I've just learned of her tragic passing."

"You were there, were you? I thought it terribly rude at the time. I couldn't possibly say anything further on the matter, of course, because it doesn't pay to speak ill of the dead. Terrible news – I read about it in this morning's papers. How can I help you, Mrs Blakely?"

"I'd like to ask you a few questions for an article I'm writing about the attack."

"Very well, but I didn't know Jane Bunton at all. I really don't see how I can help you."

"She told me she had interrupted other shows. Was that the first time it happened to you and Miss Shelley?"

He rubbed his hand across his brow. "No. Unfortunately, we were quite familiar with Mrs Bunton's outbursts. I didn't know her personally, however."

"Had you ever spoken to her?"

"Yes, a few times." He twitched his head irritably. "Forgive me, Mrs Blakely, but I'm still not clear as to why you want me to answer your questions. You attended the show, you say?"

"Yes, and I'm currently writing a review of it."

"Oh, good. A favourable one, I hope?"

"Miss Shelley is quite the performer."

"She certainly is. But I still don't see why you want to talk to me about Mrs Bunton. While it's true to say that she caused us trouble in the past, we were most distressed to hear the tragic news of her passing."

I assessed the man standing in front of me and tried to picture him with a gun in his hand. *Was it possible that he was a murderer?* I couldn't imagine so. He seemed perfectly benign, but I sensed a wariness of me. I couldn't decide whether he was simply struggling to understand why I was here or whether he had something to hide.

I decided to keep him talking in the hope he would let something useful slip. "What did Miss Shelley make of the tragic news?" I asked.

"Miss Shelley was devastated to hear of Mrs Bunton's death, as you can imagine. She's only a young woman and her nerves are fragile. She was ever so upset to learn that the poor lady had died in such a manner. The fact that Mrs Bunton was critical of her work meant nothing to her. Miss Shelley has a most forgiving nature and understands why people might question her integrity. Her abilities are so unique that it really comes as no surprise that some doubt them.

"We both understand that Mrs Bunton was an educated and intelligent woman who questioned the world around her. Neither Miss Shelley nor I bore any grudge against her whatsoever. All Miss Shelley and I can do now is hope that the culprit is caught as soon as possible."

I recalled the professor explaining that he had taken Miss Shelley into his home, and was intrigued at the prospect of meeting her. "Would it be possible to speak to Miss Shelley?"

"May I ask why?"

"I attended her show, as I've explained, and I'm keen to meet her in person. Perhaps she has a few words she'd like to share with our readers?"

He nodded in response to this remark, no doubt seeing it as an opportunity to publicise their performances.

"Very well. I shall fetch her. In the meantime, Mrs Blakely, please make yourself comfortable here." He gestured toward a plum-coloured settee. "I shall ask for some coffee to be brought in."

A short while later, Professor Mortimer returned to the room with Elizabeth Shelley. A slender young woman, she wore a charcoal-coloured day dress and her brown hair was tied in a long plait. Her face was pale and fine-boned. I detected some asymmetry in her features, but couldn't immediately establish why. I then realised that one of her eyes was dark brown and the other green.

A squat, grey-haired woman in a blue dress with a fuss of lace on the bodice, accompanied Miss Shelley. Professor Mortimer introduced her as his wife, Mrs Susanna Mortimer. She wore several pieces of fine jewellery and I suspected good money could be made from Miss Shelley's performances. I wondered how much she received herself and how much ended up in the pockets of Professor Mortimer and his wife.

Both women were unsmiling, seemingly wary of my intentions. I gave them a broad grin to lighten the mood, but it had little effect.

Miss Shelley seated herself in a chair, her hands folded neatly in her lap. Her gaze rested on me, as though she were scrutinising my soul. I tried to ignore my discomfort and told her how much I had enjoyed the show. My platitude prompted no reaction from her.

"I was very interested to hear your story," I added. "Professor Mortimer found you at St Pancras Workhouse, is that right?"

She nodded.

"That can't have been a pleasant place to be," I continued. "Do you have any happy memories of your time there?"

The girl shook her head.

I persevered. "How different your life is now," I continued. "When did you first become aware of your unusual talent?"

Her eyes shifted upward, as if she were plucking a reply out of the air. "I thought it was normal. The workhouse called Professor Mortimer in. He was the one who saved me."

"He saved you from the workhouse?"

"Yes, and he brought me here, into his family."

This response prompted a faint maternal smile from Mrs Mortimer.

"And your ability to communicate with spirits was something you had previously assumed to be quite normal?" I ventured.

"Yes, I'd always been able to do it. I thought everybody could."

Her face remained expressionless as she spoke, and there was little animation in her body. She merely sat with her hands in her lap, facing me. Her waif-like appearance and contrasting eyes were disconcerting. I felt a shiver run down my spine.

Had she always been like this? Or was she playing the part of someone else?

"Were you at the workhouse with your family?" I asked.

"I'm an orphan."

"Do you have any memories of your family?"

"No, she doesn't," interrupted Mrs Mortimer, "and it's upsetting for Elizabeth to think about them. I would appreciate it if you didn't ask anything further about her family."

This seemed an odd response from Mrs Mortimer, and I wondered why it should be upsetting for Miss Shelley to think of her family if she couldn't remember them.

"I do remember one thing," said the girl. Her face softened a little, and I wondered if she was finally about to reveal a little of her true character. "I was very young, and I was at church."

"I think the story you're about to tell Mrs Blakely was a dream, Elizabeth," said Mrs Mortimer.

"If it was, it felt very real to me. A lady at the church called me a devil."

I felt my heart skip, considering this an awful thing for someone to have said to a child.

"Why?" I asked.

"She told me I had the eyes of the devil, in front of everybody. They all stared, and I hated it." Her face coloured a little.

"What happened then?" I enquired.

"Someone asked her to leave. The vicar, I think."

"And so he should have done!"

"That's enough now," said Mrs Mortimer, getting to her feet.

She didn't like my questions and clearly wanted to bring our encounter to an end, but I wasn't ready to leave just yet.

"Jane Bunton," I ventured. "She interrupted your performance several times, and now—"

"Yes, we heard what happened to Mrs Bunton," Mrs Mortimer snapped. "It's dreadfully sad and we're extremely shocked. But we need to conclude our time with you now, Mrs Blakely. Elizabeth has another performance this evening, and she must rest beforehand."

"Absolutely," added the professor. "She cannot perform if she's tired."

"Very well," I replied. "It's been a pleasure to meet you all."

The professor escorted me to the door before the coffee had even arrived.

CHAPTER 9

I met James in Highgate that afternoon, and we walked to the cemetery together.

"We have a witness who saw a man running through the cemetery yesterday evening," said James. "It's a good place for a fleeing assailant to go in order to escape detection."

"He must be a fearless assailant. I shouldn't like to hang around here at night."

We reached the tall iron gates at the west side of the cemetery.

"Perhaps you're thinking back to the case of poor Lizzie Dixie," said James.

We had come to this spot two years previously when the famous actress had been found dead in the cemetery.

"I am," I responded. "I suppose I shall always associate this place with her tragic death."

The cemetery sloped downhill once we passed through the gates. Heavy grey clouds were rolling in from the south-west, covering the rooftops and spires of London in gloom. I could feel spots of rain in the air.

We followed a path toward a large cedar of Lebanon tree, which kept watch over those in eternal slumber beneath the monuments and headstones.

"The assailant could have headed west from here to Hampstead Heath," said James, "or continued south toward Kentish Town."

"And Camden Town," I added.

"Yes, Camden Town isn't awfully far from here."

"Can we be sure it was the murderer who was seen running through here?" I asked.

"We can't be entirely sure. But how else would you explain why someone should be running through a cemetery on a dark, foggy night? We have to consider it a strong possibility that it was the man who fired the shot."

"Have any witnesses reported seeing a young woman running away?"

"Not yet."

My mind returned to Elizabeth Shelley and the Mortimers. I told James about my visit. "They were remarkably keen for me to leave," I added.

"You're a news reporter, Penny. Very few people enjoy having a reporter in their home asking questions."

"I think they may be hiding something."

"That's interesting. I intend to speak to them myself shortly."

"You'll find them quite odd, I think. Especially Elizabeth Shelley. Her manner is most unusual for a girl of fifteen."

"She's an unusual girl," said James. "Few people can claim to be communicating with spirits on a regular basis."

"If you choose to believe that she communicates with spirits, that is. I feel sure that it's all a performance. I'd hoped to find out what she's really like. Instead, the performance continued at home."

"I can't really imagine them being frank with you, Penny,

knowing that you could publish anything unflattering they might say in your newspaper."

I understood this. "It's just frustrating that I couldn't seem to get the measure of them."

"Perhaps you don't need to."

"But Professor Mortimer may be behind the murder of Jane Bunton."

"You think he murdered her because she'd become too much of a nuisance?"

"Yes. She was challenging their method of making a living. He told me she had interrupted a number of their shows."

"But would they really murder her for doing that?"

"I don't know. Speak to them, then see what you think."

We reached a pair of tall stone monoliths that flanked a large archway. The ornate carving of the stone resembled the architecture of ancient Egypt. We were only a short distance from the location where Lizzie Dixie had been shot. I shivered, but felt a modicum of relief as we turned away from the spot and continued downhill.

"I spent some time talking with Samuel Bunton today," said James. "He seems like a respectable chap. He owns an animal charcoal factory in Whitechapel."

"He burns animal bones?"

"Yes, although he doesn't do it himself, of course. He has a factory full of people to carry out the unpleasant task. He told me a bit about it and explained that the charcoal is used in the sugar refining process. There are only a few factories in London that do it, so he always has a lot of business."

I wrinkled my nose. "It must be very odorous work."

"It must indeed. If I were you, Penny, I would stick with writing!"

"What sort of man is Samuel Bunton?"

"He's a confident fellow, which I would say is common for a man of his background and education. He has a slight arrogance about him, but I'm sure that's one of the characteristics required to run a business like his. He's in a terrible state about the events of last night, of course. Witnessing the attack on his wife was extremely distressing for him. He's not the sort of chap to go into a lot of detail, but I could see from the manner in which he spoke that he's still very distressed."

"What did he tell you about their marriage?"

"He told me it was a happy one. They had been married for three years and there were no children. He was at pains to explain that the lack of offspring had done nothing to detract from their happiness. As you already know, Mrs Bunton was a modern woman. Apparently, she was busy campaigning for several causes and wasn't the type of woman to stay at home and keep house."

"Was he happy with that?"

"Apparently so. I could find no reason to doubt that their marriage had been a happy one. That said, I'm relying solely on what Samuel Bunton has told me about it. As you know, with cases like this, a different truth often emerges over time. I had a brief word with the housekeeper today, but I should like to speak with her at greater length. Servants can be a useful source of information."

"So you've found no reason to doubt Samuel Bunton's word as yet?"

"Not yet. But I should like to speak to him again, perhaps under different circumstances. Paying someone a surprise visit sometimes yields a different result. I should like to catch him a little off guard to see how he manages my questions. Perhaps I'll pay a visit to his bone-burning factory."

I grimaced. "Rather you than me, James."

CHAPTER 10

I passed Mr Conway as I climbed the staircase to the *Morning Express* offices. He puffed past me, his large frame clad in brown tweed. He gave me a brief nod, but his expression was thunderous.

Upstairs in the newsroom, Mr Sherman was speaking animatedly to Edgar Fish and Frederick Potter. I guessed that he and Mr Conway had just had another disagreement.

"Mrs Blakely!" he said. "I do hope you have another article on the Highgate murder for me. Have they arrested anyone yet?"

"Not yet."

He shook his head. "Dreadful. That poor young woman."

"It was the same woman I interviewed for my article about Elizabeth Shelley."

"Yes, I realised that. I think we should publish the interview now, in the light of what's happened."

"You don't want me to rewrite it?"

"No, let's leave it as it is for now. Our readers will be much more interested in the interview now that the poor woman is deceased. I'd like you to obtain daily updates on the investigation, if possible. It's rather convenient that you're married to an inspector of the Yard."

I handed him my latest update, and he began to read through it.

"Very convenient indeed," said Edgar. "It seems you still manage to be handed all the best stories, Mrs Blakely, even now that you've left. In the meantime, I have to write about the new ambassador to Constantinople."

"Nothing dull about that, Fish," said the editor, looking up from the article. "Sir Edward Thornton, the second Count of Cacilhas, is a most distinguished gentleman."

"At least you don't have to spend most of your time in parliament, Edgar," added Frederick.

"Ah, but you enjoy that, Potter," Edgar replied. "You spend all your time snoozing and socialising with the politicians rather than doing any work."

"But socialising *is* work! I have to fraternise with them in order to understand the internal workings of Westminster."

"I don't think anyone will ever understand them, so there's little point in trying. Parliamentary reporting is simple work."

"Fancy becoming our new parliamentary reporter, Fish?" asked Mr Sherman. "Maybe you and Potter could exchange roles?"

"Oh, I'm not at all sure about that, sir. Some debates in parliament go on until evening. I don't think Mrs Fish would take too kindly to me being so late home."

Frederick laughed. "Simple work... isn't that what you called it? Perhaps it's not so simple after all."

"Most of my articles are far more complicated than any parliamentary debate."

"It would be best for the pair of you if you could just get

on with your assignments without arguing," said the editor. "Your deadline is four o'clock." He turned to me. "This is an excellent report, Mrs Blakely, although it's a shame to hear that so little progress has been made since the last one."

"The Yard is working extremely hard, sir."

"I'm sure of it. We need a little more, though. An interview with the husband would do nicely."

I felt my heart sink. "But he's a widower in mourning, sir. I wouldn't like to intrude on his grief at this point in time. Perhaps I could pay him a visit next week?"

"Do our readers want to wait until next week, Mrs Blakely? No, they do not! They want to read it right now. The husband actually saw who committed the crime. He can provide a tantalising eyewitness account! It's very important that you speak to him as soon as possible. This newspaper needs all the readers it can get." He glanced around the newsroom, then lowered his voice. "I need to show Mr Conway just how many copies of this newspaper I can sell. He's labouring under the misapprehension that he knows better than me. He may be the proprietor of the paper, but he knows nothing about editing it. His requests are growing more ridiculous by the second; all of them driven by one unfortunate personal circumstance or another."

"Namely, his wife and the editor of *The Holborn Gazette*," said Edgar.

Mr Sherman turned on him. "Watch it, Fish! I don't want gossip taking over this newsroom. I'm not willing to speculate on the reasons for Mr Conway's recent change in character, but—"

"It would certainly explain a few things," Edgar added.

"That's enough!" Mr Sherman barked before addressing me again. "Anyway, Mrs Blakely, the fact of the matter is, I need to do everything I can to improve circulation so I can prove Conway wrong. He needs to understand that I'm the best man for the job, and that without me..."

"There would be no *Morning Express*, sir," said Edgar.

"Thank you, Fish." Mr Sherman gave a rare smile. "That's the most sensible thing you've said all day."

CHAPTER 11

I returned to the house in Highgate the following morning to speak to Samuel Bunton. The housekeeper answered the door. A red-haired woman of about thirty, she had a freckled complexion and wore a plain black mourning dress.

"Mr Bunton doesn't wish to speak to any news reporters," she said after I had introduced myself.

"Would you mind asking him, at the very least? He could issue an appeal to the *Morning Express* readers. Someone might be able to help us find his wife's killer."

She pushed her lips together, giving this suggestion some thought. "I can ask him, I suppose."

"Thank you, and please emphasise that a bit of publicity in the newspaper could help the investigation."

The housekeeper left me waiting on the doorstep, and I instantly felt some regret about my choice of words. Although there was a possibility that an interview with Mr Bunton might assist the investigation, it was far from a certainty.

She returned a short while later and informed me that her employer had no desire to meet with me.

"That's a shame," I responded. "I met Mrs Bunton shortly before her death. I didn't know her well, but I would have welcomed the opportunity to pass my condolences on to her husband."

The housekeeper raised her eyebrows. "You met her?"

I nodded and explained the circumstances of our meeting. I noticed her eyes grow damp as I spoke. She swallowed hard before responding. "I shall ask him again."

This time Samuel Bunton agreed to talk to me, and the housekeeper showed me into a darkened drawing room. The curtains were drawn and the mirrors covered with black crepe. Shelves of books on the walls receded into the gloom.

I could only observe Mr Bunton in the flickering white glow of two small gas lamps. He was a tall, handsome man with a brown moustache and a prominent, square jaw. His eyes were small and dark, his hair neatly parted and oiled. He wore a black suit with a high collar.

I offered him my condolences.

"I'm not accepting many visitors at this time," he responded, gesturing for me to sit, "but Miss Jones tells me you're the lady Jane met with after her protest at the theatre." He gave a faint smile. "She told me all about you. She was so pleased that you were going to write an article about her."

"And I still am," I replied. "She struck me as a remarkable person."

"She certainly was." He slumped into a chair. "I miss her so much."

I chose not to respond, waiting instead for him to continue.

"It all happened so fast," he said. "That's what shocked me most; the speed of it all. I was in disbelief for some time afterwards. It felt like a bad dream that I would somehow awaken from to discover it hadn't happened after all. Only it had."

"Did you get a good look at the people who killed her?" I asked.

"Sort of. I answered the door because Miss Jones was out for the evening. We weren't expecting visitors, and I had no idea who it might be. I must admit that it startled me to see the young woman at the door. Her appearance struck me as unusual because she was wearing a hooded cape and her face was cast in shadow."

"Do you think she was deliberately obscuring her features?"

"In light of what happened afterwards, yes, but I didn't think of that at the time. She struck me as a rather ghostly figure. It was foggy, and it almost felt as though she'd manifested out of the fog. I know that makes little sense, but it's how I felt. I couldn't even tell you if she was a girl or a woman. But she was barely out of girlhood, if she was an adult.

"She asked to see my wife. I asked her name, and she replied that she was called Chloe, but no surname was given. I thought then that she was a maid of one of Jane's friends and had been dispatched with a message for her. Although the young woman seemed odd, I suspected no danger at all. I wish now that I'd asked who had sent her and requested that she lower her hood so I could see her face." He rubbed his brow. "I've thought of a great number of things I should have done differently. I can't tell you how it haunts me.

"Anyway, I came back to this very room and fetched Jane, and that's when she went to the door. I didn't accompany her because I saw no reason to do so."

"Did the name Chloe mean anything to Jane?"

"No. She looked a little perplexed, but I told her I

thought the young woman was a maid." He gave a resigned shrug. "Another terrible mistake."

"You didn't know what was about to happen," I said.

"No, but I should have asked who she was. I made assumptions, and my wife is dead as a result."

I felt he was being unnecessarily harsh on himself. "Jane is dead because of that young woman and her accomplice," I replied. "It's not your fault."

He ran a hand through his hair. "Perhaps not. But when I think of everything I could, and *should*, have done, it seems so avoidable."

"I heard Chloe ran away before the shot was fired," I said, moving the story along.

"Yes, she must have done. She certainly wasn't there when I ran out. I heard the shot, and it felt as though the entire house shook. I instinctively knew something was wrong. The blood in my veins ran cold. I've never felt that sensation before and I never want to feel it again. I ran to the door and..." He shook his head. "I couldn't believe it. Poor Jane was just lying there. She'd fallen awkwardly and her arm was twisted beneath her. That's how I knew she was badly hurt. She never would have remained in that position otherwise."

His voice choked a little, but he managed to continue. "I looked around for Chloe, and that's when I saw the dark figure at the foot of the steps. All I could make out was a long coat and a top hat. He had something in his hand, which I assumed was the gun, and he darted away in the direction of the village. I shouted after him, but in a matter of seconds he was gone.

"My attention returned to Jane. Her face was pale and her lips were a dreadful shade of blue. I tried to move her into a more comfortable position, but the blood..." He tailed off. "She told me he had a gun... her voice was so weak. I asked her who the man was, but she couldn't speak any more. Her eyes were closing. I was torn between staying with her and running after the man who had shot her.

"One of the neighbours ran up the steps, Mrs Hargreaves. I asked her to stay with Jane while I went after the murderer. I felt sure I could catch him, and I'm sure I would have done if it hadn't been for the fog. He just vanished. Melted away. It makes me so angry!" He covered his face with his hands.

I chose not to say anything, leaving him to recover from his distress.

"The neighbours got hold of a doctor," he said once he had gathered himself, "but he couldn't do anything for Jane. They kept her warm with an overcoat, but she was fading fast. I managed to get back just in time to say goodbye."

I felt a lump in my throat. The situation was almost unbearable.

"Then they took her away," he said. "Mrs Hargreaves kindly offered to clean the steps for me. I wasn't fit for anything; my senses felt completely numbed. It's still impossible to believe that I'll never see Jane again. This home we shared for three years was a place of tranquility; a place I looked forward to returning to each evening. But now it feels like an empty shell. I can't tolerate the thought that I'll never again hear Jane's voice, or feel her warm touch or embrace. The house feels so empty without her. It's as if all the lights have gone out. I've struggled to sleep since the incident and, if I do sleep, I expect to see her face before me whenever I wake. It always takes me a moment to realise that I won't.

"There's no way out of this now. This is how I'll live for the rest of my life. Everything will be empty, cold and dark. I keep turning to speak to her, expecting her to be there. Miss Jones has been of such great help to me, but no one could ever replace Jane. I'm completely bereft without her. The police simply must find the man who did this. They have to catch the pair of them! I won't rest until they do. And when they're caught, as I believe they will be, my first question to them will be, 'Why?'"

Mr Bunton expressed his sentiments so clearly that it was almost impossible not to shed a tear as I listened to his story.

"Have you any idea who might have done this?" I asked.

"None." He shook his head. "Other than... Well, I know it sounds foolish, but there's a possibility that the young woman might have been Elizabeth Shelley. And perhaps the man who fired the shot was Professor Mortimer. I really can't imagine either of them hatching such a plan; it seems quite impossible. But I suppose one could argue that the pair might have sought revenge for all the hard work Jane was doing to expose their fraudulent show. I know it sounds like a wild accusation, and I've informed the police that I cannot wholeheartedly believe the pair would do such a terrible thing."

"Why not?" I felt encouraged that his suspicions lay in the same direction as mine.

"Because it would ruin their career, wouldn't it? It would be nonsensical. That said, I really don't see why anybody would want to harm Jane."

"Her father must be extremely upset," I ventured, hoping he would tell me more about him.

"He is. Her mother died some years ago and her father, Jeremiah Wigmore, is quite elderly now. He never married again. He comes from money and lives at Farley Lodge in Dulwich Village. Jane's older sister, Lydia, died in girlhood and her younger sister, Caroline Harding, lives with her husband and children in Battersea."

"Were Jane and Mrs Harding close?"

"They were quite different, and for that reason I don't think anyone could describe them as close. Having said that, there was never any significant disagreement between them. We were in the habit of calling on Caroline and her family on the last Saturday of every month."

"How would you describe your relationship with Caroline's husband?"

"Bartholomew is quite a dull man." Mr Bunton chuckled. "But he's perfectly pleasant with it. I don't think I'm the type of person he would be friends with, exactly. The sisters differed from each other, and therefore so did the husbands. We've always made an effort with each other, though, especially now that Mr Wigmore is in such poor health."

"Oh dear, is he seriously ill?"

"He's only suffering from old age, if you can call that an illness."

"Where does the Wigmores' wealth come from?"

"Mr Wigmore's father inherited it from his father, who made his money from tar."

"Tar?"

"Up in Shropshire, where they scraped the tar off the tunnel walls. He set the business up with another gentleman, then sold his half to him. He was a very successful man who could put his hand to anything. After earning his money in tar, he opened a general store. And from there he opened several more general stores. He eventually sold those as well, so he retired with decent wealth."

"Have you visited Jane's father since her death?"

"Yes, and very tricky it was, too. No father should ever have to learn that his daughter has died. It was awfully difficult to speak to him about it. He's never been the sort of person to openly discuss a tragedy, but he's a churchgoing man, and I think he's found great solace in the church. That's the only consolation he can find at this time, I suppose. I'll admit that I haven't been very consistent with my own churchgoing over the years, but I've attended twice since Jane's death. I find that it provides some comfort. I persuaded Miss Jones to accompany me the second time.

She's awfully upset by Jane's death as well. She and Jane had developed a strong friendship."

"They were friends?"

"Yes. I realise it's unusual for a servant and a mistress to form a close friendship, but that's the sort of woman Jane was. She never judged people on their background; class differences were of little importance to her. Jane and Miss Jones – or Edith, as she knew her – shared a great love of books. Jane was quite delighted to discover that Edith had brought a trunk filled with books when she moved into the rooms at the top of our house. As soon as Jane saw the books being unpacked, she immediately started looking through them to see if there were any she hadn't read. As you can see, we have a lot of books in our home."

He gestured at the shelves on the walls. "The pair of them were always swapping books and discussing them. It wasn't long before Edith felt like a member of the family. Much like a spinster aunt, I would say. They would take walks together on the heath. Sometimes I joined them, but my work keeps me busy."

"You own a factory, I hear."

"Yes, and it keeps me pretty occupied, as you can probably imagine." He looked up and met my gaze. "Miss Jones told me you could print a public appeal for help in the *Morning Express*. Is that correct?"

"That's right. The police have already found several witnesses who saw the assailant running from the scene. I'm hoping the article will prompt a few more who saw him to come forward."

"That would be very helpful."

A knock at the door interrupted us, and Miss Jones quietly entered the room.

"I apologise for intruding, sir," she said, "but Mrs Hargreaves is here."

"Ah, yes." He checked his watch. "It's eleven already! I do apologise, Mrs Blakely, but we'll have to leave it there. Mrs Hargreaves insists on checking in on me at regular intervals." He smiled.

I thanked him and went on my way.

CHAPTER 12

"I paid a visit to Professor Mortimer today," James said at dinner that evening. "He comes across as an educated, considerate, measured gentleman."

I snorted in reply.

"Now, that's not particularly ladylike, Penny. You really do have your mind set against him, don't you?"

"Does that surprise you? I truly believe that he may have murdered Jane Bunton."

"It's a little too early in the investigation to be making that sort of assumption."

"But the description of the pair who called at the Buntons' home clearly matches the appearance of Professor Mortimer and Miss Shelley."

"Can you be sure of that? As I recall, Mr Bunton said the man holding the gun was little more than a shadow in the fog."

"He said that he was wearing a top hat and overcoat."

"I'm sure that Professor Mortimer wears similar garments. The trouble is, most gentlemen in London wear similar garments."

"But the young woman who called herself Chloe has to be Elizabeth Shelley."

"I haven't met Miss Shelley yet. She was out with Mrs Mortimer when I called on them."

"How convenient."

"You usually manage to keep an open mind with cases like this, Penny."

"I do, but I can't think of anyone else who had a credible motive to murder Mrs Bunton."

"Professor Mortimer has an alibi for the time of Jane Bunton's murder. Apparently, he was in a meeting with a Dr Corkhill at the Royal Institution."

"Has that been verified?"

"Yes. We sent a man down there, and Dr Corkhill confirmed it."

"Do you have an alibi for Elizabeth Shelley yet?"

"Not yet. I need to speak to her first. She may well have one, and then the pair can be eliminated from our investigation. Let's not rule out the possibility that someone was trying to be clever. Perhaps the people who carried out the crime were pretending to be them."

My immediate response was to laugh, but then I reasoned that similar tricks had been played in previous cases we had investigated. I gave this idea further thought. "You think someone might have been that organised about it?"

"The people who carried out this murder were incredibly organised. They chose a night when visibility was poor, and they'd obviously agreed between them how the crime was to be committed. The young woman was to call at the door, deliberately obscuring her appearance, and then she was to get well out of the way before the shot was fired."

"Has anyone reported seeing her running from the scene yet?"

"No, not yet."

"But several witnesses saw a man running away."

"Yes, three people have claimed that so far."

"But the only person who saw the young woman was Mr Bunton."

"And Mrs Bunton."

"Who's no longer here to confirm it. We only have Mr Bunton's word."

"Interesting..." A smile spread across James's face. "Do you think Mr Bunton might have concocted the story, Penny?"

"No one else has been able to back it up so far. If he'd wanted to murder his wife, he could have simply pretended that Professor Mortimer and Miss Shelley were responsible." I sat back in my chair and considered this. "On the other hand, I didn't find his manner at all disingenuous when I spoke to him today."

"Some people are highly skilled in these matters, though, aren't they? It can be difficult to spot deception if someone's particularly good at it. Like you, I found Mr Bunton to be quite genuine, and I can't see any reason why he might have wanted to kill his wife. But as you pointed out, we only have his version of events to go on. If we could find another witness, his version of events would be less questionable. Don't forget, however, that a man was seen running from the crime."

"Perhaps the man was him. He readily admits that he ran off in pursuit of the suspect. And the witnesses only reported seeing one man running, not two."

"That's because the culprit got away."

"Or was Mr Bunton just running around, pretending to chase after someone?"

"It's an interesting theory, Penny, and I don't think Samuel Bunton should be overlooked as we continue our investigation."

"We must also consider the idea that the young woman and the man with the gun were real but were perhaps only pretending to be Professor Mortimer and Miss Shelley."

"Or maybe it really was Mortimer and Shelley."

I sighed. "Once again, we have a case on our hands that becomes increasingly complicated the more we look into it." I thought of Professor Mortimer and Elizabeth Shelley again. "Miss Shelley is young," I said. "Perhaps it would be easier for you to get the truth from her than from him."

"In theory, younger people are rarely as deceptive as their older, better-practised counterparts," replied James. "But we must remember that she makes her living from deception."

"You mean Professor Mortimer makes a living from her deception."

"I don't know what the exact arrangements are between them, but I imagine Miss Shelley must be quite adept at bending the truth."

"There are so many reasons why we need to speak to her alone," I said. "First, to establish whether she had anything to do with Jane Bunton's death. Second, we need to determine whether she's being exploited."

"Exploitation is quite an extreme assumption, Penny. While I have no doubt that the professor and his wife are benefiting financially from her supposed skills, we must remember that she was stuck in the workhouse before they took her in. Anything is better than the workhouse, as you well know."

"I suppose they can't be doing anything terribly wrong if she's happy with the arrangement, but I don't like Professor Mortimer one bit."

"That doesn't mean he's a murderer."

"I know, but I don't trust a word he says."

"You can't trust anyone in an investigation of this kind."

"Who's your main suspect, James?"

"I don't have one yet. Professor Mortimer is up there, along with his young protégée. We'll also need to consider Samuel Bunton, especially if no one can verify his account that two people resembling Mortimer and Shelley called at his home that evening."

"Were you aware that Mrs Bunton came from a wealthy family?"

"Yes, Mr Bunton told me that."

"Money always causes problems," I continued. "Jane's father is elderly and in ill health – presumably close to death, even. Jane had two sisters but one died young. Only one of the three sisters is left now."

"Is she set to inherit the family fortune?"

"I don't know for sure, but it seems fairly likely."

"Another interesting fact to consider. We shall need to speak to the father and the sister."

"I only had Professor Mortimer and Miss Shelley in mind as suspects when we began this conversation," I said, "but now there appear to be several other possibilities."

"And we may find more yet. That's why I said it's too soon in the investigation to start making assumptions. In fact, making assumptions is always a mistake. Everything we decide needs to be based on fact."

CHAPTER 13

I took my latest article in to the *Morning Express* offices the following day.

"Here's my interview with Samuel Bunton," I said, handing it to Mr Sherman as he sat behind his desk.

"Who?" Perspiration glistened on his brow and there was colour in his cheeks, as though he was agitated about something once again.

"Jane Bunton's husband," I explained. "Mrs Bunton was murdered—"

"Yes, yes. I know who Jane Bunton was." He seemed irritated that he'd briefly forgotten the name and skimmed through the article. "Excellent. This will be published in the morning." He fixed me with a steely gaze. "No sign of your husband getting close to catching the culprit yet?"

"Not yet. The search has been hampered by the fact it was such a foggy night. And there may be more suspects than we first realised."

"Yes, yes. The Yard always finds a good excuse, doesn't it?"

I felt a snap of anger, knowing how difficult this particular case was proving. "It's not an excuse, sir. There's still a great deal for us to learn about Mrs Bunton."

"Well, I suppose you'd better go off and learn it, then, hadn't you, Mrs Blakely?"

He was speaking to me as though I were still an employee. But although I disliked his abrupt tone, the thought of uncovering as much information as I could about Jane Bunton appealed to me.

"Very well, sir. I must say that Professor Mortimer also intrigues me."

"Who?"

"The man who performs with Elizabeth Shelley, the medium."

"Oh, them. Yes, I know."

"Professor Mortimer may be behind this crime but, even if he's not, I should like to find out more about his relationship with Miss Shelley."

"Hmm?" Mr Sherman had been riffling through some papers on his desk while I was speaking, and I suspected he hadn't listened to a word I had said.

"Shall I go and find out all that I can, sir?"

"Yes, absolutely. Didn't I already ask you to do just that?"

"You did."

"Very well." He dismissed me with a wave of his hand. "Thank you, Miss Green."

"Mrs Blakely."

"Oh, yes. And tell that inspector husband of yours to catch this dreadful murderer as soon as possible. Our readers want to be able to put their trust in the Yard."

I left Mr Sherman's office and walked along the wood-panelled corridor toward the staircase. As I did so, Mr Sherman's secretary, Miss Welton, stepped out of her office. Tall and thin, her grey hair was tied at the nape of her neck, and she was wearing a dark woollen dress. She greeted me with a modest smile, which was customary for her.

"Is Mr Sherman all right?" I asked, keeping my voice low.

"Not really." She adjusted the pair of pince-nez delicately balanced on the end of her nose. "He and Mr Conway have had a difference of opinion."

"I heard about that. He seems quite distracted by it."

"Very distracted indeed. I suspect he's constantly anxious about Mr Conway's next visit. Mr Conway's calling in every day at the moment – sometimes even twice a day." She glanced around her, as if to make sure that no one overheard, then leaned in. "They say he's turned to the drink."

"Mr Conway?"

She nodded. "It's making life terribly difficult for Mr Sherman."

I heard his office door open behind us. "Miss Welton!" he called out. "I asked for coffee!"

She raised her voice. "I brought it in to you, sir. It's on your desk."

"Where?"

She gave me a bemused glance, then went past me. "I'll come and find it for you. It's probably gone cold by now."

As I stepped out onto Fleet Street, a chill easterly wind whipped at my coat. I wrapped my scarf a little tighter around me and made my way west toward the Strand. Ahead of me, the elaborate spires of the Royal Courts of Justice rose up into the low grey cloud.

I crossed the road and hopped onto an omnibus. I needed to head southwest to Chelsea, then cross the river to Battersea. I had no idea how I would be received by Jane Bunton's sister, Caroline Harding, but I was interested in finding out.

The Harding family lived in a three-storey, red-brick townhouse close to Battersea Park. It had been recently built, and a number of the homes close by were still under construction.

A maid informed me that Mrs Harding was at home and would receive me. I was shown into a comfortable drawing room where I found Mrs Harding dabbing at her eyes with a black handkerchief. She stood to greet me and I saw that her silk mourning dress was fashionably cut. Jewels glittered at her ears and wrists, and her cheeks were coloured with rouge. She had the same sharp nose and prominent teeth as her older sister, but her face was plump, her build large.

I offered her my condolences.

"Thank you." Her ample bosom heaved as she dabbed at her eyes again. "It's been such a dreadful time for us. Simply awful. Do please sit." She gestured to a settee occupied by a little white lap dog. "Don't worry about Tiny; she likes visitors. She won't bite you."

I didn't share her confidence as I sat down and noticed the small dog baring her teeth at me.

"Tiny!" scolded Mrs Harding. "This lady is a friend. You must be nice!"

Tiny licked her lips, then hopped off the settee and sat down at her mistress's skirts. Mrs Harding scooped her up and rested her on her lap.

"Yes, it's been a dreadful time," she repeated, dabbing her brow. "We just can't make sense of it."

"When did you last see your sister, Mrs Harding?" I asked.

"I saw her... well, it would have been about a month ago. She and Samuel came here for dinner. We had a lovely bit of partridge, that's how I remember it."

"And how did she seem then?"

"Jane? She was the same as she always was."

"Did you get on well?"

"We were quite different people, she and I. Jane liked her causes. I like causes, too, only not quite so passionately. My priority has always been my home and my family, so that's where I put most of my energies. Jane didn't have any children, so I suppose it was only natural that she had more interests outside the home. I also do a great deal outside the home, of course. I help out at the East London Hospital for Children in Shadwell. Do you know it?"

"I've heard of it."

"You simply *must* visit, Mrs Blakely, especially given that you're a news reporter. You could write something favourable about the hospital and encourage people to donate money to the cause. Charles Dickens helped an enormous deal. He wrote an article about the hospital and called it 'a small star in the east'. Isn't that a wonderful description?"

I nodded.

"Only Charles Dickens could have come up with something like that. My father met him once, you know."

I chose not to enquire about the circumstances, instead steering the conversation back to Jane. "Did your sister seem her usual self when you last saw her?"

"Absolutely. And I recall asking her, once again, if she wanted to join me in helping out at the hospital. It wasn't something she ever did. I don't know why, but that was Jane for you, I suppose. It doesn't take a great deal of effort to help, you know. I began by entertaining the children there. I read stories and brought in toys for them to play with. The East End is so desperately poor. Did you know that some of those children had never seen toys before? It's awfully sad. I resolved to bring a little light to their day, and they were enormously grateful for it."

My teeth clenched with impatience as she continued.

"As time has gone by, I've made myself an amenable companion to some of the poorest families associated with the hospital. Many are destitute and have known great suffering. Many appreciate a simple conversation or having an activity to do. I've taught embroidery and more useful skills, such as basic sewing, and much of my work is concerned with raising funds for the hospital. My husband is a town clerk, and we have countless wealthy acquaintances who have been extremely generous when I've asked them to support the hospital. We've had a very successful year so far, and have managed to raise a good few hundred pounds."

"Wonderful," I responded. "You are to be congratulated, Mrs Harding."

"Well, thank you." She gave a coy smile and patted Tiny on the head. "One does what one can."

"My editor has set a tight deadline," I said, "so I'm afraid we must conclude our meeting fairly soon."

The maid brought in a tray of coffee and cakes, which I feared would extend my stay longer than I would have liked.

"Of course, Mrs Blakely. But you will stay and have some refreshments, won't you? I can't have this all to myself."

Once the coffee had been poured, I asked Mrs Harding whether she could think of anyone who might have wished to harm her sister.

"According to Samuel, a strange professor and a young woman who communicates with spirits are responsible. I'm not familiar with either, but I understand Jane had upset them in some way. Quite typical of Jane, I must say! She didn't mind who she offended."

"She told me she had a particular dislike for mediums after your mother consulted one many years ago."

"Yes, Jane was most vexed by that. I really don't see why. Mother was convinced by the medium's abilities and felt sure she had communicated with our sister, Lydia. Whether she actually had or not is of no real consequence. It gave Mother comfort. I can completely understand that as a mother myself. Jane seemed to find all manner of provocations for her causes, but I can't say that I was particularly convinced by any of them. The trouble with speaking out about such things all the time is that it invariably leads to trouble. Jane's outspokenness directly led to her death."

"Do you think the professor and the medium could be responsible?"

"I couldn't possibly say! For all I know, Jane may have upset someone else."

"That doesn't mean she deserved to be shot, though."

"Of course not. One should be able to freely express oneself without fear of death. Murdering someone simply for speaking their mind takes us back to the dark ages."

She sighed and took a sip of coffee. "I must be frank with you, Mrs Blakely, we weren't close as sisters. Our opinions differed greatly, and there were times when I spoke to her most unkindly." She clasped a hand to her chest. "I feel terribly ashamed of that now. If only I had been kinder to her, it would have made a significant difference to the way I feel now. But I suppose one can never foresee such things. I had no idea she was about to be murdered! And now I've lost yet another sister."

Mrs Harding wiped her eyes with the black handkerchief. "I don't suppose the enormity of what's happened has fully dawned on me yet. My senses feel numb, and I find myself wandering from room to room in a daze, struggling to concentrate my mind on anything at all. I'm fully aware that my grief will grow a lot stronger in time, but at present I feel as if there's a perpetual fog in my mind."

"Have you seen Mr Bunton since Jane's death?"

"Yes, I called on him, and he was grateful to me for that. He hasn't received many visitors, although I understand his neighbour, Mrs Hargreaves, has been very kind to him. He's extremely upset about her death, as you might imagine. And then there's the housekeeper, Edith Jones. She's an odd one."

"What do you mean by that, Mrs Harding?"

"I don't think she likes being a servant. She was determined to become Jane's friend from the day she moved in. Don't you think that a little strange? A housekeeper is nothing more than a servant, whether Miss Jones likes it or not. All sorts of trouble can occur when friendships are forged between a family and its servants."

"It sounds as though Jane was happy to be a friend to Miss Jones."

"Yes! I don't understand that, either. Jane had grown up with servants, so she fully understood the boundaries that should exist between a family and those who serve it. I can only suppose that she didn't want to appear rude, but personally I would have dismissed a housekeeper who was so desperate to be my friend. It just isn't right. In fact, it's insubordination. Father never understood it, either."

"How is your father?" I asked.

"Suffering terribly, just as I am. There are only the two of us left now. Isn't that sad? He's elderly and in poor health. I was the one who had to tell him the news! I really thought he was about to fall down dead in front of me, there and then." She took another sip of coffee.

I sensed Mrs Harding was enjoying the dramatic thrust of the conversation. Perhaps she was expecting an equally dramatic response from me, but I chose not to give it. She seemed to have rather an attention-seeking nature.

"It wouldn't surprise me if Father were to die soon."

This macabre statement was difficult to ignore. "Really?"

"I'm afraid so." She stroked Tiny and gazed pitifully at the little dog. "And then it will just be me."

CHAPTER 14

The following day was a Saturday, and I met Eliza and Francis for a walk in Hyde Park.

"It's a shame James can't join us," said Eliza as we followed the path around the Serpentine Lake. The sun was out, but a brisk breeze was doing its best to remove the last of the autumn leaves from the trees.

"He's busy working on the murder case," I replied.

"That poor lady in Highgate?"

I nodded, then told Eliza and Francis about the work I had been doing on it.

"It sounds like a fascinating case, Penny," said Francis. "You always manage to find such interesting topics to write about."

"Interesting?" Eliza chipped in. "It's a murder! I don't call that interesting; I call it dreadfully sad."

"Perhaps *interesting* was the wrong word," conceded Francis, "but it's a darn sight more eventful than anything I do."

"You work in a library," responded Eliza, "and an important library at that. People need libraries, Francis. It's a respectable and responsible job."

Francis chuckled. "I suppose so. Although I had a lot more fun travelling about Amazonia in search of your father."

"That was just plain dangerous. You're lucky nothing awful happened to you."

Francis frowned. "Aren't you grateful to me for finding your father?"

"Of course I'm grateful!" she said emphatically. "Enormously so. But it was dangerous, all the same."

"And exciting. I must say that I quite like the idea of adventuring again."

"Really?"

"Yes. I missed home, but I enjoyed being somewhere so different and exploring the unknown. There's nothing quite like it, is there?"

"I suppose not," replied Eliza. "Not that Penelope and I have ever had the opportunity to do such things."

"You could do it. Why don't we travel somewhere together?"

Eliza stopped. "Travel somewhere? But where?"

"I don't know. Anywhere!"

"You're forgetting that I have children to look after, Francis."

"I haven't forgotten about them. They're looked after by their governess most of the time, aren't they? Maybe they could stay with George for a few months."

"I don't want my children staying with George!" Eliza huffed, walking on ahead.

Francis and I exchanged a bemused glance.

"Did you enjoy reading Professor Mortimer's study of Elizabeth Shelley?" he asked me.

"I'm not sure 'enjoy' is quite the right word. He certainly reports on all his experiments in great detail, but I struggle to believe that he applied the same rigour as he did in some of his earlier work. He presents his reports with a biased air, as though he already believed in her supposed abilities before he began his experiments. He should have begun with some scepticism, at the very least."

"A sensible suggestion, Penny. It's no surprise that his experiments proved his theories if his mind was already made up."

"It also seems rather convenient for him to have provided a seemingly scientific basis for an act that makes good money for him at the theatre."

"Indeed." Francis nodded agreeably. "You really do examine everything thoroughly, don't you, Penny? I'm sure very few journalists go to such lengths with their research."

"I only do it because I find it interesting."

"Natural curiosity is a wonderful gift."

He grinned as we caught my sister up, but Eliza's expression remained stony.

We stopped at the tea rooms and were shown to a table.

"One of my tenants has placed me in rather a difficult position," announced Eliza.

"Mrs Reddings?" I queried.

"No, another tenant. I swore Mrs Reddings to secrecy, but she appears to have told a friend of hers about my gift. And now the friend has asked me for a similar sum of money."

"Oh dear," said Francis.

"She's in great financial difficulty as well. I don't know whether she's a widow, but there's no husband on the scene and she has seven children. One more than Mrs Reddings! She makes a great effort to keep their home clean and tidy, doing the very best she can. Her children's hands and faces are always washed. They're sent out to the water pump in the yard first thing every morning and evening to carry out the task. Their clothes are mended and laundered as best as they can be. And yet she also has to work, leaving the older children to look after the younger ones. How can I possibly turn down her request?"

"This is what happens when people go handing out money to these people," commented Francis.

"But money is exactly what they need!"

"Of course it is. They have a never-ending need for it because our society has no intention of helping them out of poverty. You could give this lady ten pounds and Mrs Reddings another ten pounds, but will that solve their problems? I'm afraid not."

Eliza's lips thinned. "What's the answer, then, Francis?"

"Salaries. The two ladies you mention must work hard in their factories, probably six days a week. Are the factory owners poor?"

"I don't know. I shouldn't think so."

"I shouldn't think so, either. In fact, it's likely that they own more than one factory. A good number of them, perhaps. If they paid their workers a little more and kept back a little less for themselves, that would go some way to redistributing the country's wealth."

"But if workers were paid more, it would be difficult to make the factories profitable. And if that happened, people would stop running them, and then there'd be no industry at all."

"I'm not suggesting that factory owners should make no money from their businesses," responded Francis, "but they should consider the needs of their workers when it comes to paying wages. They should take into consideration the cost of employees' rent and bills. Once they've done that, they should be willing to pay a wage that covers these basic expenses. And if it turns out that someone cannot work due to sickness, the local parish should provide for them."

"You're forgetting about all those unscrupulous land-lords," said Eliza, stirring sugar into her tea. "If they know a worker is being paid a good wage, they simply increase the rent."

"There should be laws in place to stop that."

"But if you put laws in place, people won't want to become landlords any more. They need to make money, too."

"Of course they do, but I think a balance could be struck. Our present system allows some people to make a lot of money while many others are condemned to a life of poverty. Imagine if there were proper rules in place about wages and rents, and a process whereby the local parish helped those who couldn't work. Wouldn't that make everything fairer? And wouldn't it make your job easier? In fact, there probably wouldn't be a need for it at all."

"That does make sense," I commented.

"Thank you, Penny." He smiled.

"But that isn't how life works," snapped Eliza. "And if you ask me, discussing what could and should happen is a waste of time. I have tenants living in poverty who are turning to me right now for help. I've helped one, but I simply don't have the means to help any more!"

"You'll have to explain that to her," replied Francis. "But you do have my sympathy, Eliza. I know it won't be easy."

"No, it won't. I'm tempted to help her, as I did Mrs Reddings, but what if more people were to find out? They'd come calling, too. Then there's also the risk that Miss Barrington might find out, and I'd be in a lot of trouble if she did. Isn't it awful that you can get into trouble merely by doing the right thing?"

"But is it the right thing?" he asked.

"I believe it is."

"Perhaps Miss Barrington put the rule in place for a good reason," said Francis. "We don't always know what the best way to help might be. Maybe campaigning for fairer wages would be a better use of your time."

"And leave Mrs Reddings to struggle in the meantime?"

"Wouldn't it be worth it to achieve better wages for all? If Mrs Reddings brought home enough money each week, she could feed and clothe her children more easily. She could even employ a woman to help with her little ones. And perhaps her children could be supported to find better employment than working in a factory."

"That sort of thing takes years, Francis."

"You've been campaigning for women's rights for a long time, Eliza. That demonstrates to me that you have plenty of patience when it comes to the causes you support. I don't see why this one should be any different."

"Because I can see people suffering who need help now."

"Why not discuss it with Miss Barrington?" I said. "Perhaps she'd have some ideas."

"It's too late for that. I've already broken an important rule by giving the money to Mrs Reddings."

Francis and I exchanged a glance.

"What was that look for?" asked Eliza.

"We don't have any answers, I'm afraid," I said.

"Yet you both seem to agree that I've made a terrible mistake."

"I do think it was a mistake," said Francis as kindly as he could. "But I understand why you did it."

They both looked to me, and I felt pressured to comment.

"It's a difficult situation, Ellie," I said, trying to be as tactful as possible. "I don't know how I would have managed the situation if it had been me."

"I think you would have found yourself in exactly the same situation, Penelope. No one in their right mind can stand by and do nothing when they see others struggling. Anyway, I can see that I'm never going to find a solution by discussing it with you two. Let's plan our trip to Liverpool instead, seeing as it's only three weeks away now. Have I told you that Mrs Garnett is going to join us, Penelope?"

"No," I replied. "That is a surprise."

Mrs Garnett was my former landlady, from whom I had rented a room for several years. My father had taken the room for a while after I left, and he and Mrs Garnett had formed a close friendship.

"The more the merrier, I suppose," I added.

Eliza gave a humourless nod and Francis's expression appeared strained.

I sensed that all was not well between them.

CHAPTER 15

Edith Jones answered the door when I called at Samuel Bunton's house for a second time. Her red hair was tied neatly back from her face and she was wearing a plain mourning dress.

"Oh, hello again," she said. "I'm afraid Mr Bunton isn't home at the moment."

"That's all right," I responded. "It was you I wished to speak to, Miss Jones."

"Me?"

"Do you mind?" I moved up a step.

"No, but I don't see what you would want with me. You're a news reporter, aren't you?"

"Yes, but I won't publish anything from our conversation. "I only want to find out a little more about Mrs Bunton."

The housekeeper's expression softened a little. "I see. Well, I suppose you'd better come in."

I stepped into the hallway.

Miss Jones glanced around her. "I don't know where we could talk. Would the kitchen do?"

"The kitchen will do just fine."

I followed her down to the basement and into a large kitchen with whitewashed walls. Gleaming pots and pans hung from hooks on the ceiling. A table and chairs had been positioned in front of the hearth.

"The cook's not here at the moment," the housekeeper explained, "and the maids are above stairs."

We sat opposite each other at the table.

"How can I help you?" she asked.

"I'd like to know more about Jane," I said. "The more I learn, the better an idea we'll have of who murdered her."

"Isn't that the job of the police?"

"Yes, it is, but my husband happens to be an inspector at Scotland Yard."

She raised her eyebrows. "And you're helping him?"

"In a way. I've reported on several murder cases over the years, and I suppose I have found myself helping him from time to time."

"How interesting! I think Jane would have enjoyed a profession like yours. She was so clever." Miss Jones lowered her eyes. "But he wouldn't allow her to take any paid employment."

"Mr Bunton, you mean?"

Miss Jones nodded. "But there's nothing anyone can do about that now, is there?"

"I hear you were good friends with Mrs Bunton."

"Yes, I was. I know it's unusual, but we had a lot in common. I miss her terribly. I don't know what the future holds now, but I felt so fortunate to have found this position. I was quite unhappy with my previous family, so I'd responded to a number of adverts in the newspaper. There was always a risk that I'd find myself in another position I didn't enjoy, but even though I was offered places with several other households I was determined to wait until the perfect position came along. And then it did." She smiled.

"Mr Bunton told me you shared a love of books."

"We did! Jane Austen and Walter Scott were among our favourites. We enjoyed many happy hours discussing their work. Our friendship began with books, but then we discovered we would talk together on many other topics, too. We sat down at the end of each day, and she would tell me about her activities and show me the latest leaflets she'd written and had printed. She was always busy – she cared so passionately about a great number of topics. She was always interested in hearing what I thought, and I would help her with her plans and ideas. She sometimes joked that she was paying me to be a companion rather than a housekeeper."

She paused and wiped her eyes. "When you meet someone who views the world in much the same way as you, you gain a soulmate. There was never any complication in my work as Jane's housekeeper. She was a fair employer, and I was respectful of her position as lady of the house. I feel so blessed to have known Jane. My life was truly enriched by her."

It struck me that the housekeeper spoke more fondly of Jane than her own sister had.

"Can you think of anyone who might have wished to harm Mrs Bunton?"

"The obvious answer would be Professor Mortimer and Miss Shelley. They certainly match the description of the people who called here that evening. Even so, I can't imagine the two of them carrying out such a horrific act. It's one thing to be a fraudulent spiritualist, but it's quite another to commit cold-blooded murder. I'm wondering if it was a case of mistaken identity."

"You mean you think they were after someone else?"

"They must have been."

I recalled Mr Bunton telling me that the young woman

had asked for Jane by name, but I chose not to mention it. "Is there anyone else who comes to mind?" I queried.

"There's no doubt that Jane must have annoyed various other people. I know that she wrote to a school for mentally infirm children and told them they should allow the little ones out into the yard for exercise, just as other schools do. The headteacher was livid! He even called at the house and told Jane to mind her own business. But he wouldn't have murdered her over such a thing. No one in their right mind would have done so."

"How did Mrs Bunton get on with her husband?"

Her face stiffened. "It's not my business to say, Mrs Blakely. You must understand that I feel a great loyalty toward my employer."

"But the fact that he forbade her from taking paid employment presumably caused some disagreement between them?"

"I wouldn't know about that. She said very little about her husband to me."

"Did you overhear any disagreements?"

"Occasionally, but disagreements often occur in marriages, as I'm sure you well know. Jane was happy, and that's what mattered the most."

"Of course, and I'm glad that's how you're choosing to remember her. But it's only by examining all aspects of her life that we can determine who might have wanted to harm her."

"Not Mr Bunton, if that's what you're suggesting!"

Miss Jones scowled at me, and I realised I was beginning to lose some of the rapport I had established with her.

"It's just that you knew Mrs Bunton so well, Miss Jones, and I value your opinion."

She responded with a smile, then her face grew serious again. "Please tell your husband to catch the people who did this," she said. "They mustn't get away with it. No one will ever understand what I've lost." Her face crumpled, and her head sank into her hands.

I waited patiently as she composed herself. I couldn't find any words of comfort; Jane's death seemed too senseless for that.

Eventually, Miss Jones righted herself and dried her eyes. "I can't tell you how it feels to wake each morning with the realisation that this awful thing has actually happened. It feels like a suffocating weight on my chest, and at times I feel as though I can't breathe properly."

I rested my hand on her arm, hoping it would be of some comfort to her.

She fixed me with her wet eyes. "Your husband really must solve this case, Mrs Blakely. And you must do everything you can to ensure that he does."

"I will," I said with resolve.

"Nevertheless, nothing can bring Jane back," she continued. "That's the real tragedy. She was the truest friend I ever had."

CHAPTER 16

J ames and I lunched together at the Old Castle Coffee and Dining Rooms in Highgate.

"It's all the wrong way round," I said.

He looked up from the menu. "What are you talking about?"

"Jane Bunton's sister had very little to say about her murder. She talked about herself most of the time. Meanwhile, the housekeeper, Miss Jones, was as upset as you'd expect a member of Mrs Bunton's family to be."

"Mrs Bunton didn't get on well with her sister, but she got on well with the housekeeper. That's all there is to it."

"I understand that. It just struck me as odd when I spoke to them both. I don't think I've ever seen a servant so attached to her employer."

"And yet it happens."

"I suppose it does. Miss Jones wouldn't be drawn on her opinion of Mr Bunton, unfortunately. I couldn't decide whether she was hiding something or whether she simply chose not to discuss her feelings about him from a sense of loyalty."

"What did you ask her about him?"

"I was trying to find out if the Bunton marriage was a happy one."

"I'd like to know the answer to that myself. Samuel Bunton hasn't given much away on that topic, either. Did you ask the sister about it?"

"No, but I don't think she would have known. They don't appear to have been close, and I can't imagine Mrs Bunton confiding in her. If she confided in anyone, it would most likely have been Miss Jones. But I'm sure there are many things she hasn't told me."

"I imagine you're right. Did she mention the money?"

"What money?"

"Mrs Bunton lent her some money."

"How much?"

"One hundred pounds."

"That's a large sum! I wonder what it was for."

"Mr Bunton thought it might have been for Miss Jones's mother, who was apparently in great financial need. He wasn't happy about it, however. In fact, he only found out about the loan after it had been given."

"Miss Jones mentioned nothing of that to me! It's a shame, because I thought we got on rather well today."

"People don't tend to mention these things, though, do they? There's often a great deal of shame involved when it comes to borrowing money. And the relationship between the two women was clearly a personal one. Mr Bunton didn't even know about it initially."

"Was the loan ever repaid?"

"Samuel Bunton doesn't believe so."

"In which case, there's a possibility that Mrs Bunton requested a repayment and Miss Jones was struggling to pay it back."

"There is indeed. And it may have caused a falling out between the two women."

"She didn't admit to anything of that sort."

"She wouldn't, though, would she? She'd have wanted you to think all was well between them."

Although I knew James was right, I felt disappointed that Edith Jones had deliberately kept something from me. I had found her likeable, and I had unwittingly fallen into the trap of trusting her word a little too much. I knew it was a weakness of mine. Many years of journalism had trained me to be a natural sceptic, but I couldn't help placing my trust in people with whom I developed a good rapport.

"Did Miss Jones tell you where she was when Mrs Bunton was murdered?" he asked.

"No."

"You didn't ask her?"

"No, I didn't. I suppose I thought it would sound rather accusatory. And it never occurred to me that I needed to establish an alibi for her because I didn't think she would ever have considered murdering her beloved employer. Now you've told me about the money, I wonder if she might have had a motive after all."

"It's only a possibility. Don't trouble yourself too much over it, Penny. I need to interview her, anyway, so I'll ask her for an alibi then. It's my job, after all."

My mind was beginning to dwell on another possible scenario. "Perhaps Mr Bunton and Miss Jones conspired together to murder Jane," I suggested. "I know it sounds foolish, but we should consider every option. That might explain why Miss Jones didn't want to talk about him. Perhaps she was worried about accidentally giving something away."

"If they conspired to murder her, the only motive I can think of is a romantic affair between the two," he said. "I would consider it unlikely, but that doesn't mean it didn't happen."

"I'll be interested to hear what you make of Miss Jones," I said. I thought about how upset she had been by the end of our conversation and how genuine she had seemed. I wanted to believe what she had told me, but it was becoming increasingly difficult to do so.

"I'm quite worried about Eliza and Francis," I said, changing the subject.

"In what sense?"

"Eliza is impatient for him to propose."

James groaned.

"Why did you respond like that?"

"She's only just obtained her divorce. What's the hurry?"

"I don't believe there's any great hurry, as such. She'd just like to know what Francis's intentions might be."

"I'm sure he'll propose in time. The poor chap's just preparing himself. It's not a matter to be taken lightly, is it?"

"No, but their courtship has been going on for quite a while."

"Not particularly. It began when he returned from Colombia, did it not? That was only five months ago. Give the man a chance, I say."

"The trouble is, Eliza needs to know sooner rather than later if he doesn't intend to propose."

"So she can find another husband instead?"

"I don't know. Possibly."

I thought of our most recent meeting and how Francis had spoken of travelling, while Eliza wouldn't even entertain the idea. Their interests appeared to be diverging.

"I think Eliza just needs to give him a little more time," said James. "Let's not forget that it wasn't so long ago that he wanted to marry you. He's had to change his allegiances quite significantly."

I felt heat in my face once again. "That's all forgotten about now. It's not at all relevant."

A waiter approached and asked if we were ready to place our order.

"Not quite yet," replied James. Once the waiter had left, he turned back to me. "It wouldn't surprise me, Penny, if Francis still holds a torch for you."

"He does no such thing!" The heat burned fiercely in my cheeks. "Please don't talk like that, James. You're my husband! Any fondness Francis had for me in the past is long forgotten about."

"For you, perhaps. But if I imagine myself in Francis's shoes, he has my sympathy. The sister he loved married someone else, and that left him with the other sister, who..."

"Be careful what you say about my sister!"

"Yes, absolutely." He returned to the menu.

I took a deep breath and tried to cool myself. Any mention of Francis's past fondness instantly made me feel tense and uncomfortable. The trouble was, I suspected there was some truth in what James had said. There was a twinkle in Francis's gaze and a smile on his lips whenever we met. And although I loved James wholeheartedly, I had always harboured a sisterly fondness for Francis. *Was it possible that his feelings for me were delaying his proposal to Eliza?* I pushed the thought from my mind, feeling embarrassed and ashamed to have briefly entertained it.

CHAPTER 17

M y discomfort had eased by the time James and I ate our breakfast the following morning. Yet I felt tired, and had little interest in my toast, which sat on my plate, half-eaten.

"What's wrong with your breakfast?" James asked.

"Nothing's wrong with it," I replied. "I just have very little appetite this morning." I took a sip of tea and found it equally unsatisfying. "I can't help but wonder why a man as educated and accomplished as Professor Mortimer has chosen to involve himself in spiritualism."

"That's why you're not interested in breakfast, is it? You're dwelling on the case. It helps to forget about it occasionally, Penny, otherwise it'll keep you awake at night. I've experienced that a few times myself."

"I just can't understand whether spiritualism is something he genuinely believes in or whether it's all a ruse to earn a bit of money. I struggle to believe that he'd be in desperate need. Surely a scientist of his calibre would be well remunerated?"

"If he's still doing any real scientific work, that is."

"Perhaps he isn't. But the money must have been good, so why pursue something entirely different?"

"Is it possible that there's more money to be made through the theatre performances?"

"Maybe, but surely he risked ruining his reputation by making the change. What must his former colleagues make of this new line of work?"

"That's something you'd have to ask them."

"And so I shall. What's the name of the man who provided him with an alibi?"

"Dr Corkhill, at the Royal Institution."

"Good. Then that's who I shall speak to."

The Royal Institution, a scientific organisation, was housed in a grand stone building on Albemarle Street in the heart of Mayfair. Its imposing, classical facade was lined with a row of towering stone columns.

I approached the entrance with a falter in my step, slightly intimidated by the proud-looking intellectual establishment. Places like this conveyed a sense that lower status visitors were unworthy to step through its doors.

I asked for Dr Corkhill at the reception desk. After a brief wait, it surprised me to discover that he was willing to see me. I presumed he was curious to discover what a news reporter might want with him.

I found him seated in a dingy room lined with shelving. Books and scientific apparatus occupied the shelves, and a tall worktable stood in the centre of the room. The air had a distinctly medicinal scent.

Dr Corkhill was a white-haired man with a moustache that had been waxed into a horizontal shape and pointed at each end. He directed me to a pair of worn chairs beside the fireplace.

"Professor Mortimer, you say?" He turned his left ear toward me, as if he were hard of hearing.

"Yes."

"Joseph?"

"Yes."

"What of him?"

"How long have you known him?"

"How long have I what?"

I eventually managed to encourage Dr Corkhill to tell me about his colleague.

"I first met him about thirty-five years ago at the Royal College of Chemistry. Hold on, I think it's closer to forty years now. Isn't it astonishing how quickly time flies? It'll be forty years next year. I remember he was an extremely studious young man, and rather clever, too. A serious chap, though – you couldn't have much of a joke with him. Not that I'm prone to be a joker myself, but he was always the serious sort. You know the type I mean, I'm sure.

"Mortimer was fascinated by crystallisation and studied the supersaturation of salt solutions. He had wonderful fun in his laboratory creating a variety of crystallised structures, some of which were quite beautiful, I should add. Then, sixteen years ago, the great Russian chemist Dmitri Mendeleev published his Periodic System. In it, he described all the known elements. He wasn't the first to do this; John Newlands had already done something similar a few years previously. However, what made Mendeleev's system noteworthy was the fact that it enabled him to predict three more elements that hadn't yet been discovered. Quite remarkable, wouldn't you say?"

I nodded.

"Well, you can imagine what happened next among some of us chaps. There was an urgency to be the first to discover the new elements Mendeleev had named: eka-boron, eka-aluminium and eka-silicon. Mortimer was particularly keen on eka-aluminium and spent a great deal of time examining quantities of sphalerite extracted from a mine in Cumbria."

I nodded again, hoping his explanation would soon reach its conclusion.

"Unfortunately, a Frenchman got there before him," he continued. "Lecoq de Boisbaudran in 1875. He named the element 'gallium' after the Latin for Gaul, his homeland. Ekaboron was then discovered by a Swede called Nilson and is now known as 'scandium', after Scandinavia, of course. Did you spot that? Nilson claimed he knew nothing of Mendeleev's prediction, which irritated Mortimer immensely, as you might imagine. There he was, hoping to discover one of the missing elements when chaps like Nilson were working away at it, completely oblivious of the prediction. Eka-silicon is the only one that remains undiscovered, though I believe Mortimer has lost all interest in the challenge now. Have you read any of his work on sphalerite?"

"I haven't."

"That's a shame."

"What do you think prompted his interest in spiritualism?"

"In what?"

"Spiritualism," I repeated. "He's taken a young woman into his charge; a medium called Elizabeth Shelley."

"Oh yes, Elizabeth Shelley."

"What do you think about that?"

"Well, I suppose it's all well and good if you believe in such things, but it sounds like a lot of nonsense to me."

"A scientist usually works with facts and evidence, doesn't he? I found it surprising that a man from such a scientific background would put his faith in spirits and supernatural phenomena that cannot be proven."

"Yes, it does seem like a strange departure from his previous work."

"Does that surprise you?"

"Surprise me? Oh, no. Nothing surprises me these days."

"You don't think there's anything unusual or alarming about Professor Mortimer's interest in spiritualism?"

"Not at all. The man is free to choose what to spend his time on. It was a bit of a fashion for a while, wasn't it? There was some sort of society set up for it. I suppose there's a society for everything these days. If you ask me, it's just an excuse for people to get together over dinner and talk a lot. Not my sort of thing, but I've no objection to anyone else doing it."

"Have you seen Professor Mortimer recently?"

"I have, actually. He paid me a visit last week."

"Last week?" I realised this would have been before Jane Bunton's murder.

"I think so. Or was it this week? I think it might have been this week. In fact, I had a policeman here yesterday asking questions about him. That's quite a coincidence, isn't it? Young chap, he was, and rather green about the gills. Nevertheless, he wanted to know when I was with Mortimer, so I told him. He hasn't got himself into any sort of trouble, has he?"

"No, although he had a slight acquaintance with a woman who was recently murdered."

"Murdered? Good grief! That's another thing you get a lot of these days. I'm sure Mortimer had nothing to do with that."

"What do Professor Mortimer's former colleagues make of his interest in spiritualism?"

"What do they make of it? I suppose some must be rather intrigued by it."

"Is there a possibility that it might have damaged his reputation?"

"In what sense?"

"Is Professor Mortimer still considered an influential scientist?"

He chuckled. "Few scientists are considered influential, Mrs Blakely. There are a lot of us about. This building's filled with them!"

I smiled, hiding the frustration I felt at not receiving any direct answers to my questions. Then I thanked him for his time and readied myself to leave.

"Thank you for visiting me. It's been a pleasure. You're a Girton lady, are you?"

Girton was a women's college at the University of Cambridge.

"No," I responded, wondering whom he thought he had been speaking to. "I'm a reporter for the *Morning Express* newspaper."

"That's right. Forgive me! We're seeing more members of the fairer sex within these walls nowadays, and the last one I met was from Girton. A news reporter, are you? You don't look like one."

I smiled again. "You're not the first person to have told me that."

CHAPTER 18

I left the Royal Institution and walked through St James's Park to the underground railway station on the far side. A grimy fog was descending, and the upper branches of the trees were already lost in it.

Dr Corkhill hadn't struck me as a reliable alibi. His hearing was poor, and I wondered if he had understood everything the policeman interviewing him had said. His memory was also a little vague, which was understandable for a man of his age. My conversation with him had done nothing to convince me that Professor Mortimer could be ruled out as a suspect. I recalled the professor's story of how he had met Elizabeth Shelley and felt the need to explore its veracity.

I travelled along the Inner Circle Railway and disembarked at King's Cross. My walk to St Pancras Workhouse took me down a road between St Pancras and King's Cross stations. The iron cylinders of the gasworks rose to my right and several railway lines passed overhead. Grubby-faced men lingered by the gate of the Kings Cross coal depot, where coal from the north was brought in by train and unloaded onto barges and carts. Industry and its noise surrounded me, and I felt dust in my throat.

Hurrying on, I reached St Pancras Gardens and enjoyed some respite as I walked through the small, pleasant park. It had once served as the graveyard for St Pancras Church, which stood close by.

Beyond the park stood the tall red-and-brown-brick workhouse. The administration block was easy to identify with its large sash windows set in bays. The blocks that housed the unfortunate residents were noticeably plainer, the windows smaller.

As I climbed the steps to the entrance of the administration block, I wondered who might be able to help me with my enquiries about Elizabeth Shelley. If she had been a resident here for a reasonable length of time, she was likely to have attended lessons. Workhouses were legally obliged to provide schooling for a few hours each day.

A pale-faced man with a drooping moustache was seated behind a polished desk in the reception area. I introduced myself and asked to speak with the schoolmaster or mistress.

"May I ask what it's regarding?"

"I'm interested in learning more about a girl who was once a resident here. By all accounts, she now possesses psychic powers, and I should like to speak to someone who knew her to find out what they remember."

His eyebrows lifted. "Psychic powers? I don't recall anybody here having such a thing."

"Perhaps someone else might recall something of the kind?"

He huffed through his nose. "They might, but I'm sure I would have heard of the girl myself. News like that would have travelled fast."

"It's possible that she was never here at all, but I'd like to establish the facts. Would you mind enquiring for me?"

"I can speak to Miss Milton. She's the schoolmistress." He glanced up at the clock on the wall, then scratched at his temple. "I don't see any reason why you shouldn't accompany me. Then you can ask her the questions yourself."

"Thank you. I'd appreciate that."

I followed him along a corridor and through a doorway at the far side of the block. We stepped out into a courtyard and headed toward another brick building.

"Looks like the fog's coming in again," he commented, glancing up at the gloomy sky. "I expect this'll be the weather every day now until March. April, even."

His melancholic conversation and the glum surroundings depressed my mood a little. I took a deep breath and tried to force some cheer into my mind. Perhaps I was about to discover something useful about Elizabeth Shelley.

We stepped through a doorway that led into the next block and walked along a whitewashed corridor. The odour – a combination of stale perspiration and carbolic soap – was familiar to me from my visits to Shoreditch Workhouse. We appeared to be in the women's block. Sunken-faced ladies in drab workhouse uniforms eyed me as they passed by.

I was led up a narrow wooden staircase. We climbed two flights, then walked through a set of double doors.

"Here's the schoolroom," my companion said, knocking on a door.

It was opened by a small, upright woman with dark, wide-set eyes. Her brown hair was pulled back from her face and her expression was stern. She had the composure I would expect from a strict schoolmistress.

Glancing over her shoulder into the room, I saw several lines of sullen-faced children seated at shabby wooden desks.

"This is Mrs Blakely," the man said. "She's a news reporter, and she'd like to speak to you about a former pupil."

"Is that so?" She looked me up and down. "I'm in the

middle of teaching the children at the moment, so I cannot be detained for any longer than two minutes."

"Two minutes is ample time," I responded.

"Very well." She nodded at the man. "Perhaps you can step in there and watch them for two minutes, Mr Watkins. They're copying down the letters from the blackboard."

Miss Milton remained in the corridor with me while Mr Watkins stepped inside the classroom.

I explained why I was here, and that I wished to learn more about Elizabeth Shelley.

She shrugged in response. "Elizabeth Shelley? I don't recall the name."

"Perhaps her name has been changed," I suggested. "She's performing as a medium these days, but I was told that she lived in this workhouse for a while."

"When might that have been?"

"She left about three years ago, but I'm not sure how long she was here. She's fifteen years old now and lives with a gentleman called Professor Mortimer and his wife. Apparently, mysterious tapping sounds were heard in the classroom during her time here. Objects moved around the room, seemingly of their own volition, and a bench once moved around with a group of children sitting on it."

Miss Milton laughed. "I've never heard of such a thing!"

"Were you working here three years ago?"

"Yes. I've been teaching here for six years."

"And you don't recall the name?"

"No."

"Nor any child with supposed psychic abilities?"

"No! And if any child here had exhibited such abilities, I would have immediately consulted the workhouse priest and asked him to perform an exorcism. Tapping noises and things moving about the place? It sounds quite terrifying! If I saw any sign of strange behaviour in a child I wouldn't have them in my schoolroom."

"Are there any records I can look through to check for her name?" I asked.

"There are indeed, and Mr Watkins can assist you with that. I should add that several children with strange habits have passed through these doors, so I'm quite accustomed to coping with unconventional behaviours. But a child with supernatural powers..." She shook her head. "I've never encountered it, nor do I ever hope to."

Mr Watkins escorted me back to the administration building and introduced me to the clerk. He was a round-faced, bespectacled man called Mr Robinson.

Once we were in his office, Mr Robinson opened out a large leather volume where the names of workhouse inmates from three years previously were recorded.

"Elizabeth Shelley, you say?" He ran a fat forefinger down a column of sloped handwriting. "A child, was she?"

"She was here until 1882," I replied, "and she's fifteen now."

"In which case, she'd have been twelve back then. Was she here with her family?"

"I understand she was an orphan."

"Oh, right. There's a mark in this column here if they're orphans."

I waited patiently as he looked through the records. I would have preferred to save him the time and look through them myself, but he didn't seem willing to allow me near the book.

"Nothing here," he replied. "No Elizabeth Shelley. I've checked for Lizzie, Beth and other shortened variations, but none matches up with a Shelley. We have a separate record for the school. I'll have a look at that for you."

"Thank you. That's extremely helpful of you."

A short while later, Mr Robinson confirmed that he had no record of an orphan by the name of Elizabeth Shelley. I wondered whether Professor Mortimer had changed her name. If so, I had no hope of finding out her previous name unless I asked him for it.

The alternative explanation was that the professor had concocted the story because it sounded more interesting to a theatre audience than the truth. *If that were the case, who was this young woman known as Elizabeth Shelley? And where had she come from?*

CHAPTER 19

"I think Dr Corkhill is an unreliable alibi and that Professor Mortimer is a liar," I announced to James at dinner that evening.

"Goodness! Strong words from you tonight, Penny."

"Have you spoken to Dr Corkhill yet?"

"No."

"You should. And you should begin by asking him which day of the week it is. I suspect he'd be unable to tell you."

"But he's a scientist, so he must be a man of intelligence."

"A clever man whose mind and body are beginning to fail him," I responded. "It's extremely sad, but it happens."

"And what makes you think Professor Mortimer is lying?"

"I couldn't find anyone at St Pancras Workhouse who was able to corroborate his claims. No one there had ever heard of Elizabeth Shelley. She's not listed in the records, and no one could recall an orphaned child with psychic abilities. The question is, why would the professor lie about her origins?"

"Perhaps the intention was to create an exciting story for the purposes of the show? Maybe the answer is a mundane one and she is, in fact, his daughter."

"Oh, no. I don't think she is."

"What makes you so sure?"

"She doesn't look like him or his wife. And she seems quite uneasy in their company."

"That doesn't mean she's not their daughter."

"I feel certain that she isn't. She began to relate a story to me about being at church with her mother when a woman told her she had the eyes of the devil."

"How cruel."

"Some people are really quite unpleasant! However, the interesting part of the story is that Elizabeth mentioned her mother. Therefore, Mrs Mortimer cannot be her mother."

"I see."

"And, what's more, Mrs Mortimer quickly curtailed the conversation after Elizabeth divulged that story, as if she were worried that something even more inconvenient might be given away."

"Very well. It's a mystery, then."

"One that needs solving, don't you think?"

"I'm more interested in finding Jane Bunton's murderer."

"I realise that, but we should also try to find out where Elizabeth Shelley came from. If she wasn't an orphan from the workhouse and the Mortimers aren't her parents, how did they become her guardians?"

"I don't know, Penny."

"Perhaps she's being held against her will?"

"She's fifteen years of age. She could simply walk away from them if she so wished."

"She may be too frightened."

"Of an old professor and his wife?"

I felt a snap of irritation. "You think I'm being foolish."

"No, I don't. What makes you say that?"

"You seem unwilling to discuss the matter sensibly with me."

"I am willing! I'm just not sure what else you want me to say."

"You should take a closer look at Professor Mortimer."

"We *are* taking a closer look! Don't forget that the only description we have of the murderers appears to match with that of Mortimer and Miss Shelley."

"But you need to look into everything about him. We need to know where he really found Elizabeth."

"I'm not sure how relevant that is to our murder investigation."

"It may not be relevant, but something untoward may have occurred. Isn't that important enough to investigate?"

"There's no evidence that any crime has been committed against Miss Shelley, Penny. She may not be Professor Mortimer's daughter, but he and his wife have clearly taken her in and cared for her—"

"And forced her to perform on a stage!"

"By all accounts, she has a gift."

"You don't really believe that, James. Professor Mortimer has coached her into performing her supposed skills. I'm convinced it's all a ruse to make him some money."

"He is making money, but so is Miss Shelley."

"How do you know she sees any of it?"

"She's provided with a home and board, which I imagine is all she needs at this stage in her life. I'm not suggesting everything is perfect in the Mortimer household – probably far from it – but for the time being, I need to concentrate on Jane Bunton's murder. Professor Mortimer and Miss Shelley are still suspects, of course. Perhaps the wife was also involved. I hope we'll discover, during the course of our investigation, why Professor Mortimer chose to fabricate Miss Shelley's history. But perhaps he merely did so to concoct an exciting story he could tell on stage rather than for any nefarious reason."

I realised James's job was a difficult one, but it frustrated me that he shared little of my concern for Elizabeth Shelley. I felt the need to make further enquiries myself.

"Perhaps the theatre manager might know something," I said.

"Theatre manager?"

"The manager of the Theatre Royal Drury Lane. Elizabeth Shelley performs there on a regular basis. He might be able to give me more insight."

CHAPTER 20

I travelled to Covent Garden by omnibus the following morning. As I approached the theatre, I felt a twinge of discomfort when my gaze fell upon the spot where Jane Bunton and I had met. Ten days had passed since her death, and little progress had been made in finding out who was responsible.

I asked to speak to the proprietor, Richard Fairchild. He had recently replaced Sebastian Colehill, the manager I had spoken to about the murder of Lizzie Dixie two years previously.

Mr Fairchild agreed to see me in his office, the walls of which were papered in deep red. Paintings of various theatrical scenes hung on the walls in gilt frames.

I found the proprietor reclining in a chair behind a mahogany desk, puffing on a pipe. He had wavy hair, streaked with grey, and a rectangular face with full lips. A twitch raised the left side of his thin moustache at regular intervals. It also caused his left eye to narrow, which gave him a shifty expression. I wondered whether this might be an indication of his character, or whether it was mere misfortune.

"Jane Bunton made a real nuisance of herself," he said after we had made our introductions. "But that doesn't mean she deserved her tragic fate, of course."

"I was here when she interrupted Elizabeth Shelley's performance," I said. "Had she done that sort of thing before?"

"Yes, on two or three occasions. I told my men we would detain her and summon the police the next time it happened. I had been quite tolerant on the first few occasions, but the interruption last week caused me to lose my patience."

"Did you speak to her?"

"No, my men dealt with her. I rarely get involved in these things unless it's absolutely necessary."

"What did Elizabeth Shelley and Professor Mortimer make of the interruption?"

"They were angry, as you might expect. Joseph – as I know him – had strong words with me about manning the door during a performance. She shouldn't have been able to get inside and disturb proceedings in that manner."

Mr Fairchild's use of Professor Mortimer's forename suggested he knew the man well. "How long have you known Professor Mortimer?" I asked.

"About a year and a half. I first saw the girl, Miss Shelley, at a dreadful little theatre in Somers Town. It was the best venue the professor could find at the time. I suppose I shouldn't be too disparaging; the man had a lot to learn about the world of theatre. It's proved quite a change for such an eminent scientist!"

"Quite a change indeed. I'm interested to discover how Professor Mortimer came across Miss Shelley."

"A workhouse waif, she was."

"Was she really? I visited St Pancras Workhouse but found no one who could recall her ever being there. Neither could I find any record of her living there."

"Perhaps you went to the wrong workhouse."

"I recall the professor saying that it was St Pancras."

"Perhaps it was, or perhaps he was mistaken and got confused with another workhouse. Islington, for example."

"Do you know for sure that she was at the workhouse?"

"That's what they told me. Why should I doubt it?"

"No reason, I suppose."

"Exactly. And one might even ask why it matters. What really matters is that Elizabeth Shelley has an extraordinary gift. She fills this theatre every time she performs – and it's quite a theatre to fill, wouldn't you say? It's one of the oldest and grandest in London. There's been a theatre of sorts on this site for more than two centuries. It's quite something."

"And the relationship between Professor Mortimer and Miss Shelley gives you no cause for concern?"

"Concern? Why should I be concerned?"

"I wondered whether Miss Shelley might be taking part in these shows against her wishes."

He laughed. "I have never seen any sign of coercion."

I explained that I had met Miss Shelley while Mrs Mortimer was present, and that she hadn't been allowed to speak freely with me.

"The young woman is just shy," he responded.

"Have you spoken much with her?"

"No, not a great deal. It's not in her nature to speak much, aside from when she's on the stage. That's not unusual for a performer. Many are shy and retiring off stage."

"Do you think she's simply a performer rather than a genuine medium?"

"She's both! She is also a charming young woman, and a rather popular one with our audiences."

"Audiences who pay money."

He laughed again. "That's right."

"Professor Mortimer must make good money from the performances."

"After I've taken my share, the remaining proceeds go to him. He must pay Miss Shelley out of that. I can't say that I know what the financial arrangement between them is, but I know that the professor's dutiful wife attends to Miss Shelley's every need, and that they provide her with full board." He frowned. "I hope you don't mind my saying so, Mrs Blakely, but you seem to be a sceptical young woman. But whether you choose to believe in Miss Shelley's powers or not, I see no cause for concern here."

"My concern is that she's being forced into all this."

"I should think she would be able to tell someone if she were being forced to go on stage against her will. You can't force a young woman to perform like that! She has an exceptional talent, and she enjoys what she does."

"Can you be sure that she enjoys it? I'm not sure I've ever seen her smile."

"That doesn't mean she isn't enjoying her work." He slapped his palms down onto his desk, clearly growing impatient with the conversation. "I don't see why you're bothering me with all this. If you have concerns, you should raise them with Professor Mortimer directly. Or better still, ask the young woman herself."

"I shouldn't think I'd be allowed to speak to her without one of the Mortimers present."

"You could try. I'm not sure what you're trying to establish here, Mrs Blakely, but I'm afraid I can't be of any further help. I've already suggested that you speak to the Mortimers and Miss Shelley directly. They're the only people who can answer your questions truthfully."

I was tempted to comment that they had shown no sign of speaking truthfully so far, but I chose not to extend the conversation. "When is Miss Shelley's next performance here?" I asked.

"It's interesting you should ask that, Mrs Blakely, because we've just arranged a performance for tomorrow evening. And it'll be a particularly special one."

"In what sense?"

He leaned forward, a smile on his face. "Elizabeth Shelley will attempt to contact the spirit of Jane Bunton. Isn't that marvellous?"

Unease shifted in my stomach. "How macabre," I commented.

"Not if the spirit of Jane Bunton is able to tell us who took her life. Wouldn't that be something? I think you should join us."

CHAPTER 21

"Are you all right, Penny?"

These whispered words startled me as I sat at one of the desks in the reading room. I looked up to see Francis, his eyes concerned behind the lenses of his spectacles.

I sighed. "Not really." I'd been trying to draft my latest article for the *Morning Express,* but I couldn't stop dwelling on the morbid show Richard Fairchild was planning with Professor Mortimer and Elizabeth Shelley. "Some people are simply repugnant," I commented.

"They certainly are. Has someone upset you?"

"Not directly – or intentionally, for that matter – but they're planning to do something extremely distasteful, and it shouldn't be allowed."

"Oh dear. Well, I'm not sure exactly what you're referring to. The mind boggles!" He checked his pocket watch. "I'm due to finish in a few minutes – I have the afternoon off."

"Really?"

"Yes, I take every other Wednesday afternoon off. It's in lieu of every other Saturday afternoon I'm obliged to work."

"I see."

"Perhaps we could take a little stroll and you can tell me more about it?"

I smiled. Francis's caring and trusting manner was the perfect antidote to Richard Fairchild's disinterest.

"Very well."

Francis and I took a stroll through Bloomsbury Square a short while later. The fog and drizzle of recent days had cleared to make way for sunshine. Two gardeners were raking up piles of brown leaves from the lawns as we walked along the path through the square.

I told Francis about my concerns for Elizabeth Shelley and the forthcoming attempt to contact the spirit of Jane Bunton.

"What a lot of silly nonsense!" he commented. "I can't understand why anyone would think it's real."

"I agree," I said, "and it's disrespectful. Jane Bunton's memory should be respected, not exploited. What an awful thing for her family to have to endure!"

"These people are unscrupulous. All that matters to them is selling tickets."

We reached a bench and sat down.

"I wonder what Mrs Bunton's poor father will make of it," I said. "By all accounts, he's elderly and infirm. As if the shock of his daughter's death isn't enough, he now has to cope with the fact that the event is being used for public entertainment."

"It's awfully unsavoury."

I thought of Jane Bunton's sister, Caroline Harding, and wondered what she would make of the show. As someone who appeared to harbour minimal affection for her sister, perhaps she would not be overly bothered. I wondered what

Mr Wigmore was like. "I'd like to meet Jane's father," I said. "He lives in a large house in Dulwich Village."

"Dulwich is a pleasant place."

"What's the time?"

Francis checked his watch. "It's almost one o'clock."

"I could get there within an hour."

"You're planning to go now?"

"Yes. I can draft my article on the train."

"Do you mind if I come with you?"

I laughed. "Isn't there something else you'd rather do?"

"Not really. I was planning to study an interesting book I've found on the Aztecs. But seeing as it's a sunny afternoon, I feel I could really make the most of it by taking a little excursion over to Dulwich."

The walk to Ludgate Hill station took twenty-five minutes. I viewed this as the perfect opportunity to establish what Francis might be feeling about my sister and their future matrimony.

"I wonder what we'll all be doing a year from now," I said as we walked along the busy thoroughfare of High Holborn. It was a leading question, but I hoped Francis wouldn't discern the inference behind it.

"Will a great deal have changed between now and then?"

"It might have done. A lot can happen in a year, can't it? This time last year I was unmarried!"

"That's true. A lot has changed for you, Penny. And you live in the agreeable suburb of St John's Wood now, far away from the city and its smoke."

"Yes, that's another change I'm still growing accustomed to. I miss living amid all the chaos."

"I can understand that."

"What do you envisage for yourself?"

"That's an interesting question. I suppose if I work hard, I might earn myself a promotion at the library. Whether that's a fully fledged ambition for me or not, I couldn't really say."

"Do you want to work at the library until the end of your career?"

He laughed. "No, I certainly shouldn't like to be there for the rest of my working days."

"Not even if you were head librarian?"

"I must admit there was once a time when I aspired to oversee the reading room at the British Library. That's quite the job! But ever since my return from Colombia, my ambitions have altered a little."

"I thought you enjoyed your job."

"I do. I'm never happier than when I'm surrounded by books. At least, that's what I used to think. And then I went on a big adventure."

"But you were pleased to be home."

"Absolutely. I was thrilled to be home, in fact. And I made it just in time to see you married."

A pause followed. I waited for Francis to continue, but he didn't.

"What do you consider you'll be doing a year from now, in that case?" I ventured.

"I'm not sure. Perhaps I'll still be at the library, or perhaps I'll have had enough of it by then."

I decided to be more direct with my questioning. "What about marriage?"

"Marriage? Well, yes. I should like to be married." He turned and caught my gaze. "Why are you looking at me in that way, Penny? You seem to be expecting me to say more."

"I suppose I am," I responded. "After all, you and Eliza seem rather fond of each other."

"Are you suggesting that I should propose?"

"That's not for me to suggest. I merely wondered whether it was something you were planning to do."

"I..." he rubbed at his brow. "I hadn't given it a tremendous deal of thought, really... My acquaintance with your sister only really began when I returned from my travels. I knew her a little before I left, of course, but I didn't know her particularly well. Since then we have become better acquainted, and I must say that I find her company quite delightful. She has, however, been navigating difficult divorce proceedings until recently, and I felt it best to maintain some distance until that matter was resolved."

"It is now resolved, to my knowledge."

"Yes, I suppose it is. But it's still very recent."

"It hasn't been an easy time for Eliza."

"Absolutely not. I'm afraid I know little of the courting etiquette after a divorce. When is it appropriate to make one's feelings toward a divorced lady known? After a year? Two, perhaps?"

"I don't think there's any fixed rule. Besides, Ellie was estranged from George for some time before he petitioned for divorce."

"There is that to consider, I suppose."

"Perhaps the two of you need to have a frank conversation about the future."

"Yes, perhaps we do."

"I suspect Eliza would appreciate it."

"Have you discussed this with her?"

"No." I was uncomfortable telling this small lie, but I didn't want Francis to learn that Eliza and I had been talking about him and the possibility of marriage.

"I shall mull it over."

"That sounds like a good idea."

We walked on and turned right into Chancery Lane. I knew Francis could be reserved, as many gentlemen tended to be. But I detected no great enthusiasm from him about a prospective marriage to my sister. I hoped, for Eliza's sake, that I had misread the signs and he remained keen.

I worked on my article as the train took us from Ludgate Hill toward the village of Dulwich. We disembarked after a pleasant journey that lasted around fifteen minutes.

Francis took a deep breath as we walked along the platform. "The air already feels cleaner out here!"

From the station, we made our way along Gallery Road toward the village centre. Numerous large homes nestled among the trees and parkland.

"The Dulwich Picture Gallery," announced Francis as we passed the single-storey gold-brick structure. "Have you ever been inside?"

"I'm afraid not."

"A visit there is always a few hours well spent. It was designed by Sir John Soane about seventy years ago. Funnily enough, we passed near his former home on the way to the railway station. Did you notice that?"

"I didn't," I said with a smile. I was continually bemused by Francis's encyclopaedic knowledge.

"His home is now a museum, of course. Have you ever been?"

"No."

"You've never been to Sir John Soane's Museum? What do you do with your time, Penny?" He laughed.

"I really should make more of an effort to visit these places."

"You don't have to; I know you're a busy woman. I can certainly recommend them, though."

The houses were smaller and clustered closer together as we reached the centre of Dulwich Village. Among them sat several larger properties.

"We need to find Farley Lodge," I said.

"Let's ask this lad," said Francis.

He stopped a delivery boy on his bike, who pointed us toward a three-storey, dark-brick house behind a pair of tall gates. It was Georgian in style, and probably in age, too, with large sash windows and a columned porch.

"What a splendid place," commented Francis as we approached the gates. "Is this where Jane Bunton's father lives?"

"Yes, and it was once her family home. She told me a medium visited her family here when she was a girl."

"And put her off spiritualists for the rest of her days?"

"Yes, that's exactly what happened."

Francis surveyed the house again. "The elderly father is infirm, you say?"

"Apparently so. Mrs Bunton's mother died some years ago."

"Who will inherit the house after his death?"

"Only one of his children remains. Jane's sister, Caroline."

"She's set to inherit this place, then, unless the family follows the old tradition and it passes to the closest male heir. A cousin, perhaps?"

"It would be interesting to find that out. Jane was older than Caroline, and it may have been the case that Jane was set to inherit the house single-handedly."

As I contemplated this, the polished green door of the house opened and a large lady in an oversized black hat and a fur-trimmed coat stepped out. A small white dog was tucked under her arm.

"Oh goodness, it's her!" I said in a low voice.

"Who?" whispered Francis.

"Caroline Harding."

"Jane's sister?"

"Yes."

"You don't seem terribly pleased to see her."

"I can't say that I warmed to her when we met."

"Mrs Blakely?" Mrs Harding placed the dog on the ground and made her way over to the gate.

I forced a smile onto my face.

"This is quite the surprise," she continued. "What are you doing here?"

She stopped on the other side of the gate without opening it. Our conversation was clearly to be conducted through the bars. Tiny poked her head out and sniffed at us.

"I was hoping to speak with your father," I said.

"He's not at all well today, I'm afraid." Her mouth sank down into her double chin.

"I'm sorry to hear it."

"Certainly not well enough for visitors."

"I see. Well, I'm sorry to have disturbed you."

"What did you want to speak to him about?"

"I was hoping to include a few words from him in an article I'm writing about Mrs Bunton's death."

"I'm sorry that won't be possible. It's terribly nice to see you again, and to meet your husband." She nodded at Francis.

"Oh, he's not my husband. This is my good friend, Francis Edwards."

"A good friend, eh?" She beamed at Francis. "How delightful."

The smile didn't reach as far as her eyes, and I detected a glint of contempt.

"We shall leave you in peace," I said. "I hope your father recovers quickly."

"Thank you, but I doubt he will. He's taken a real turn for the worse, you see. I doubt he'll even make it to the end of the week. I don't know what I shall do without him."

"I'm very sorry to hear it."

I wasn't sure what else to say. Despite the sadness of her words, her expression remained nonchalant, her eyes dry.

"I can assure you that my husband is working extremely hard to crack your sister's tragic case," I added. "I do hope it will be solved soon."

"Hopefully, although I shan't be holding my breath." She bent down to pick Tiny up again. "Good day to you, Mrs Blakely. Mr Edwards."

She turned on her heel and walked toward a garden at the side of the house.

"I must say that I agree with you, Penny," commented Francis. "I didn't warm to her at all."

CHAPTER 22

"Francis accompanied you to Dulwich, did he?" asked James that evening. "Why?"

"He had a free afternoon."

"How very convenient."

I detected a note of envy in his tone. "What do you mean by that?" I asked.

"Convenient that he didn't have to work – unlike the rest of us, slaving away."

"There's no need to be so sullen about it."

"I'm not being sullen."

"Yes, you are. Anyway, I found it an excellent opportunity to ask him about his future plans regarding Eliza."

"Why would you do that?"

"Because Eliza wants to know whether he intends to propose or not."

"Why doesn't she just ask him herself?"

"She can't do that, James! It wouldn't be proper. And besides, I didn't ask him outright. I just steered the conversation round to the topic."

"Well? Is he planning to propose?"

"I don't know."

James raised an eyebrow. "Having second thoughts, I suppose. It's difficult to contemplate marriage with someone when the true object of his affections is standing right beside him."

"James! That sort of comment is entirely unnecessary!" I felt a flush of hot anger.

"But we all know it's the truth, don't we?"

"No, we don't! Please try to forget about the past, James. It's totally irrelevant now. I don't keep bringing Charlotte into our conversations, do I?"

"There's no need to. We never see her, and she's probably happily married to someone else by now. But with Francis..."

"He no longer holds any affection for me and, even if he did, he would never speak of it or act out of turn. He likes and respects you, and he speaks of our marriage with great reverence."

"Good for him."

"Now you're being churlish and acting like a schoolboy."

James laughed. "A schoolboy?"

Tears welled in my eyes as I left the room. I brushed past Mrs Oliver and took the stairs two at a time. I slumped into the chair at my writing desk and rolled a sheet of paper into my typewriter. I had work to be getting on with, and I had no time for James's pettiness.

I jabbed at the typewriter keys, but the tears blurred my vision until I couldn't see what I was typing. I sat back in my chair, sobbed, and pulled my handkerchief from my pocket. It was then that I spotted Tiger resting in the easy chair. She stretched out her front paws and yawned.

"Why does he do it?" I said to her. "Why does he continue to resent Francis? Francis is a good man. He's always been so loyal and supportive. And while I'm aware that he was once in love with me, it's Eliza he cares for now."

Tiger's eyes widened, as though she had her doubts about this last statement.

"He no longer loves me," I continued, "I'm sure of it. And he knows I've always been in love with James. Although, I have to say, I often wonder why when James behaves this way. He has nothing to fear from Francis. Francis is merely a good friend. You don't meet many people like him, though, do you? I don't see why I should have to avoid him just to appease my husband."

Tiger yawned, curled up, and nestled her face into the tip of her tail. I envied her ability to enjoy such a comfortable, carefree existence.

"I'm sure you have all the answers," I said, "and you'd tell me them if you could, wouldn't you?"

I held my breath as I heard James's footsteps on the stairs. He gave a gentle knock at the door before entering.

"Hello," I said curtly.

"Who are you talking to?"

"The cat."

"I see."

"She isn't rude to me."

"No, I don't suppose she is." He took a step toward me, a meek smile on his face. "I'm sorry, Penny. You were right. I was behaving like a schoolboy."

I smiled and felt fresh tears in my eyes. "Not exactly a schoolboy."

"Oh, but I was. My behaviour was immature and I shouldn't have said what I did. Francis is a decent chap and I suppose I was just a bit envious that he had a free afternoon to take a little jaunt over to Dulwich with you."

I laughed. "It wasn't all that enjoyable! We encountered Mrs Harding when we got there."

"I should like to speak to her. She sounds intriguing."

"That's one way of describing her. She was adamant that she didn't want us speaking to her father."

"Understandable, perhaps. If the old chap is frail and mourning the loss of his daughter, he probably doesn't want a news reporter and her librarian friend visiting him and asking probing questions."

"Yes, that's true. I thought it was worth a try, though."

"And it was."

"Caroline is now the sole heir to her father's fortune, unless he's decreed in his will that it be left to someone else."

"That's interesting. Yes, I suppose that Jane's tragic death means the inheritance would no longer need to be shared," he said.

"Could Caroline have murdered her sister, do you think?"

"Samuel Bunton claims it was a man who fired the shot."

"Her husband, then? Or someone she paid to carry out the attack?"

"It's not entirely inconceivable. But what of the young woman who called at the door?"

"Caroline's daughter, perhaps?"

"I think Samuel Bunton would have recognised his niece. And besides, is Mrs Harding really atrocious enough to involve her own daughter in the attack?"

"It would be a particularly cruel thing to do, but we can't rule it out."

"The young woman could even have been someone in need of money, whom Mrs Harding persuaded to be part of it," said James. He sighed. "We need more witnesses. We really need to identify the pair who called at the house that evening. While you were in Dulwich, I interviewed the Buntons' housekeeper, Edith Jones."

"How did it go?"

"It started off well but became a little trickier when I mentioned the money she had borrowed from Mrs Bunton.

She was reluctant to acknowledge it to begin with, as though she were ashamed."

"Did she say what she needed it for?"

"She mentioned that it was for her family, but she was rather vague. I suspect she'd got herself into a spot of financial difficulty. She hadn't paid any of the money back by the time of Jane's death."

"Had the lack of repayment caused any disagreement between them?"

"Not according to Miss Jones, but we only have her word for it. Jane was quite equable about the repayment terms, apparently."

"I don't suppose Miss Jones was about to admit that there was any trouble between them."

"It wouldn't look good, would it? Especially as she has no alibi for the time when Jane was attacked."

"Where did she say she was?"

"On her way to a talk at the local library. I sent a man down there to verify that she attended, and the librarian confirmed that she arrived at a quarter-past seven – fifteen minutes after Jane was murdered. It wouldn't have been impossible for her to carry out the attack and arrive at the library a quarter of an hour later."

"But we've already established that Mr Bunton saw a man with the gun."

"Yes. In which case, perhaps she enlisted the help of someone else. Remember that it was dark and foggy. A woman dressed in men's clothing might have passed for a man in those conditions. It's happened before."

"It certainly has. And the young woman?"

"The same situation may apply here as the one we considered in relation to Mrs Harding. Perhaps someone was paid to help." He sighed. "Unfortunately, we have numerous suspects and very little evidence."

The bell rang for dinner.

"There we go," said James. "Food at last. Would you like to have dinner with me, Penny, or would you prefer to stay up here and talk to the cat?"

I stood, took his hand and kissed his cheek. "Dinner would be lovely."

CHAPTER 23

I took my latest article in to the *Morning Express* offices the following day. Mr Sherman, Edgar and Frederick were engaged in an intense discussion when I arrived in the newsroom. Catching sight of the serious expressions on their faces, I offered to return later.

"No, it's quite all right, Mrs Blakely," said Mr Sherman. "You're quite welcome to join us. Let's not forget that you worked at this newspaper for ten years."

"Thank you, sir." I retrieved my article from my bag. "I've written an update on the Jane Bunton murder."

"Thank you. In fact, your timing is impeccable, Mrs Blakely. I've just informed Edgar and Frederick that Mr Conway has dismissed me from my post."

It took me a moment to fully comprehend his words. "You're leaving, sir?"

"Yes. Today."

"No!" I protested. "You can't do that!"

"My sentiments exactly," agreed Edgar. "But you'll be back again, won't you, sir? You've left before and returned."

The editor shook his head. "I won't be returning while Mr Conway is the proprietor, I'm afraid. The man has lost his senses. This newspaper's had its day."

"But it can't have!" said Frederick. "This is the *Morning Express*. It will always be the *Morning Express!*"

"That may be so, and it'll limp on, I'm sure. Under the expert leadership of Mr Conway's nephew, Crispin Childers." Mr Sherman gave a sarcastic smirk.

Mr Childers had stepped into Mr Sherman's place the previous year when our editor and a group of men had been arrested for soliciting to commit an unnatural act at the Hammam Turkish Baths in Soho. Uncharacteristically for Mr Conway, the proprietor had shown great compassion toward Mr Sherman regarding this matter. It seemed that times had changed.

Mr Childers's brief spell at the helm of the *Morning Express* had been disastrous, and I was surprised that Mr Conway had taken the same risk again. It seemed, however, that his judgement had become clouded.

"I suppose blood is always thicker than water," I commented.

"Yes, it is," responded Mr Sherman.

"If you're going, sir, then so am I!" announced Edgar.

"And me," Frederick chipped in. "I'm not sticking around and answering to Childers."

"Miss Welton won't stay, either," added Edgar. "Nor will any of the compositors or printers. They'll all walk out. Childers will be running the place on his own."

"It's a desperately sad day for the *Morning Express*," I said. "I can't believe Mr Conway has chosen to ruin his own newspaper."

Mr Sherman turned to me, his eyes moist. He held out his hand for the article. "Thank you for all your help over the years, Mrs Blakely. This will be the last edition I put together."

A lump grew in my throat, and he patted my arm in consolation.

"But I shall ensure that I make it the very best one," he said reassuringly.

CHAPTER 24

I sat in the auditorium at the Theatre Royal Drury Lane with James that evening. Scarlet and gold curtains covered the stage, and the light from an enormous chandelier highlighted the gilded plaster moulding on the balconies.

"I'm not looking forward to this," I said. "It's distasteful and disrespectful."

"It's just an act," he replied.

"I realise that, but they're exploiting Mrs Bunton's tragic death. And if it turns out they were responsible for her murder, it's absolutely abhorrent."

"I agree, Penny, but it's in our best interests to remain calm and see what they have to say for themselves. Perhaps they'll let something crucial slip."

"Such as?"

"I've no idea... just something crucial. *Anything* crucial. At this stage, I'm desperate for clues. Wouldn't it be wonderful if the performance gave us something?"

"I don't see how it would."

"While I'm fairly certain that Miss Shelley is a fraud, I do wonder whether it might be worth consulting someone with psychic abilities."

"Really? Do you think some people genuinely have these powers?"

"It's often said that some people are in possession of a sixth sense, isn't it? There could be something in it."

"I don't know if I can believe that."

"I don't mean that they actually converse with spirits; I think that's bunkum. But having the ability to hear or see something beyond our normal realm... I think that's a possibility, isn't it?"

I recalled Francis's story about the ghostly footsteps. He believed that he had encountered something otherworldly, despite his pragmatic nature. "I suppose there could be a possibility," I conceded. "I'm willing to keep an open mind about it. But when someone turns it into entertainment in order to make money from it, I'm inclined to view it as a fraudulent act – just as Jane Bunton did."

The chandelier dimmed and a spotlight flicked on Professor Mortimer striding onto the stage. His buoyant manner irritated me. He didn't seem to care one bit about Jane Bunton's death.

Once the applause had subsided, he clapped his hands together and began. "Ladies and gentlemen, I am so profoundly grateful to you all for attending this exceptionally special show tonight. As you are no doubt aware, Miss Shelley and I have found ourselves caught up in a truly awful incident. A young woman was tragically murdered on her doorstep just twelve days ago, and for no fathomable reason a finger has been pointed at us. People are claiming to have witnessed seeing us outside the house on that fateful night. People even claim to have seen me with a gun in my hand, which I apparently pointed at Mrs Bunton before firing a bullet at her." He shook his head. "It's absolutely preposterous! This is one of the reasons why Miss Shelley and I, with the help of her spirit guide, Sally Moulin, are determined to make contact with Mrs Bunton tonight. For the very first time, Mrs Bunton will reveal who truly took her life!"

I sighed as more applause rippled around me. It felt so wrong that Professor Mortimer would seek to benefit from this tragic event, drawing people to a macabre show from which he would inevitably make a lot of money. Part of me wished I could get up and walk away; I didn't want to witness this dishonest spectacle. Another part of me wanted to stay and experience the full extent of his depravity.

When all was quiet, he clapped his hands together and invited Elizabeth Shelley onto the stage. The solemn young woman strolled out of the wings and joined him at the centre of the stage. Further applause sounded, and the professor took a bow. Miss Shelley remained impassive, staring out at us all.

"Here is a girl who requires no introduction at all," the professor announced. "You are all fully aware of the powers Miss Shelley possesses, which is why you're here tonight, of course. But never before has a medium made contact with the spirit of a victim of such a heinous crime. We never imagined such a tragedy would befall us, but now, endowed with the powers Miss Shelley possesses, we must do everything we can to solve this mystery. And I tell you, ladies and gentlemen, that solve it we shall! For anyone here who has never attended our shows before, or who doubts her abilities, I must ask you to cast aside all preconceived notions and make yourself comfortable in your seat. Appreciate the spectacle that is about to unravel!"

As he had done at the previous performance I had attended, Professor Mortimer led Miss Shelley over to the curtained booth. The velvet curtain was pulled aside and she seated herself in the chair.

"For the benefit of sceptics and doubters," he said, "I shall now tether Miss Shelley to this chair so that she cannot leave it until the séance is over."

Once again, her ankles and hands were tethered, and the red silk pillowcase was placed over her head.

"Goodness!" whispered James. "What on earth's going on?"

"It gets even better than this," I commented snidely.

The curtain was drawn across, and Professor Mortimer appealed for silence. Then he stepped to the side of the stage, the lights dimmed and a spotlight appeared on a curtain at the other side. So far, the performance had been identical to the previous one. I couldn't understand why anyone would want to see it more than once.

After a long pause, there was movement behind the curtain.

"Who goes there?" Professor Mortimer called out.

"Surely he knows," whispered James.

There was a little more toing and froing with the moving curtain before the woman in white appeared.

"It's magic!" said James sarcastically.

"Shush!" said the man sitting next to him.

"Who are you, Sally Moulin?" asked Professor Mortimer.

"I am no one."

"But surely you must be someone."

She slowly raised her hands until they were held out in front of her, her palms facing the audience. "She's here," she announced.

"Who is?"

"Jane."

"Jane?"

"Jane Bunton."

James put his head in his hands. "Oh, good grief."

"Can you speak to her?" the professor asked Miss Shelley.

"I shall try."

A long silence followed; presumably a tactic they employed to increase the suspense.

"Ask Jane what happened to her," said Professor Mortimer.

"She says that she was shot," Miss Shelley replied after a short pause.

"Ask Jane who shot her."

"It was a man with a gun."

"But who was he?"

"She didn't see his face."

"But she knows who it was, doesn't she?"

"She tells me I'm looking directly at him."

Professor Mortimer glanced out at the audience. It was a quick, panicked movement that seemed a little out of character. I wondered if this reply had genuinely surprised him.

He recovered himself. "Let's be clear about this. Are you telling me, Sally Moulin, that Jane's murderer is in this room?"

"She says he's here. And she doesn't want to be here because he is present. She wants to leave."

"Tell us his name!" came a shout from the audience.

Both Professor Mortimer and the ghostly Sally Moulin started at this, clearly irritated by the interruption.

The professor stepped toward the audience. "Do not call out!" he hissed. "Any interruption is liable to stop the show!"

Sally Moulin retreated toward the curtain, as if her appearance were about to end.

Professor Mortimer turned to face her. "Is there nothing else she will tell us?"

"He is here!" she rasped again. "Protect yourselves, for he is here!" She dashed back behind the curtain.

Professor Mortimer stood still, momentarily stunned. It was unclear whether this brief performance had gone to plan or not.

"We have no control over the appearance of Sally Moulin," he told the audience. "Like you, ladies and gentlemen, I am bitterly disappointed that she was unable to name the man who murdered Jane Bunton. But you all heard what she said. He sits here among us now!" He spread his arms, as if to embrace the audience. "He is here now, in our midst!"

The auditorium filled with chatter. People glanced around at one another, debating whom the murderer might be.

Professor Mortimer seemed happy for the muttering to continue as he paced around the stage, hands behind his back. I presumed he was allowing Miss Shelley time to change her clothes and return to her seat in the booth.

Eventually, he asked for calm. "Let us see what Miss Shelley makes of this."

He pulled back the curtain to reveal the young woman still tethered to the chair, her head bowed beneath the pillowcase. She appeared not to have moved the entire time.

"Miss Shelley, I shall now awaken you from your slumber," he said, gently removing the pillowcase.

She lifted her head and shook it, as if waking herself up from a short sleep.

"Did you hear what Sally Moulin had to say for herself?" he asked.

Miss Shelley shook her head, seemingly baffled.

"Apparently, the murderer sits among us." He gestured at the audience again. "All we can do now is inform Scotland Yard of this, and every man in this audience will need to be questioned. We have done all we can, Miss Shelley. Oh, if only we could have identified the culprit! But at least we know that he is here with us tonight. I would urge everybody to watch themselves carefully, for he may be armed with his weapon of choice. I think for the safety of Miss Shelley and myself, we must leave this stage promptly, lest he launch an attack upon us."

He quickly untethered her hands and ankles, then turned to the audience again. "Ladies and gentlemen, I apologise for the brevity of tonight's performance. However, I am sure you understand that, for our own safety, we must leave the stage at this very moment. The theatre staff will notify Scotland Yard, and I'm confident that you will do everything you can to help our hardworking detectives catch the villain who carried out this most heinous act. I bid you goodnight."

There was a small, hesitant ripple of applause as he and Miss Shelley left the stage. James and I remained seated as the people in the surrounding seats stood and began to leave.

"What a lot of nonsense," he said.

I nodded in agreement. "It's absurd. I wonder how many people in the audience believed it."

"I think we need to go backstage and have a word with them."

CHAPTER 25

Once James had shown his warrant card to a theatre attendant, we were taken through a door and down a flight of steps into a cold stone corridor.

The theatre manager, Richard Fairchild, was talking with Professor Mortimer at the door of the dressing room. Their conversation paused as we approached.

"Mrs Blakely," said Mr Fairchild. "And..."

"This is my husband, Detective Inspector James Blakely of Scotland Yard," I said.

"We've already met," said Professor Mortimer.

"Yes, we have," replied James. "And Mrs Blakely and I have just witnessed your fascinating show."

"I wasn't aware that the Yard would be present tonight! That's high praise indeed. I take it you've detained all the men in the audience?"

"How many people does this theatre hold?" James asked the manager.

"A little over two thousand."

"Let's assume half of them are men," replied James,

turning back to the professor. "I don't think I could single-handedly detain a thousand men."

"Then he'll have got away!" exclaimed the professor.

"Perhaps he has. But only for this evening."

"How can you be so sure?"

"Because there are other ways and means of tracking down a murderer, Professor Mortimer. Consulting a spirit is not a common convention."

A smile spread across the professor's face. "But a novel one, don't you think?"

"Certainly very novel."

"It was a bold decision to focus on Mrs Bunton's killer, Professor," I said. "Who do you think was responsible?"

"It was certainly someone in the audience, but that's all I can tell you. If that's all the spirit of Jane Bunton wished to impart to us, there's little more we can do about it."

"We'd like to speak to Miss Shelley, please," said James.

"She's rather tired, I'm afraid. She always is after a performance."

"I understand that, but I'd like to speak to her all the same."

"Very well."

The professor stepped aside so we could enter the dressing room. We found Elizabeth Shelley seated on a chair by the mirror, wide-eyed, with her hands in her lap. I still couldn't quite accustom myself to her non-identical eye colour. Next to her sat the squat form of Mrs Mortimer in a purple dress, the bodice festooned with countless tiny bows.

James introduced himself to the pair. "That was some performance," he said to Miss Shelley. "And to think that Jane Bunton's murderer was sitting in the audience just now! How unsettling."

The young woman nodded.

"Can you remember where you were when Jane Bunton was murdered?" he asked.

"She was at home," replied Mrs Mortimer. "We both were."

"I should like Miss Shelley to answer, please."

"Why? She's shy and I can speak for her. We were both at home in Camden Square."

"Is there anyone else who might be able to vouch for that?"

"Ask the servants."

"Very well. Your address?"

Miss Shelley sat silently while Mrs Mortimer gave him the details, the girl's hands fidgeted in her lap.

"When did you last see Jane Bunton, Miss Shelley?"

The girl hesitated, then seemed to gather her thoughts. "I saw her being removed from here last week."

"Did you speak to her?"

"No, I only saw her from a distance. She was at the back of the audience and they took her out."

It seemed surprising that Miss Shelley had seen her at all from her position on the stage with the lights shining down on her.

"Did you happen to see her after she was removed from the theatre?"

"No."

"How would she have?" interrupted Mrs Mortimer. "She never had anything to do with Jane Bunton."

"Did you ever meet Jane?" James asked Miss Shelley.

"I met her once. That was... Oh, I don't know how long ago it was. Last year, I think."

"And what were the circumstances of your meeting?"

"She spoke to me after a show."

"What did the two of you speak about?"

"I didn't say much. She told me I was a fraud." There was little expression in Miss Shelley's voice. She didn't appear to have taken offence at being condemned as a fraud.

"It was an extremely unpleasant encounter," added Mrs Mortimer. "Mrs Bunton was exceptionally rude to us. Imagine speaking to a young woman in that manner! A girl, in fact. It was most upsetting."

Professor Mortimer entered the room, presumably having just finished his conversation with the theatre manager. "Do you have everything you need now, Inspector?" he asked.

James leafed through his notebook. "I'm not sure."

"I paid a visit to St Pancras Workhouse a few days ago," I said to the professor. "I wanted to find out what they remembered of Miss Shelley there."

"Why would that be of interest to you?"

"I supposed that a girl with abilities as unusual as Miss Shelley's must have caused quite a stir. The story of the waif from the workhouse is rather a fascinating one."

"Good."

"The trouble was, I couldn't find anybody there who remembered Miss Shelley," I said. "They had no record of her at all."

"That's because she's changed her name."

"From what?"

"I'm not at liberty to say. That's a private matter for Miss Shelley."

"Even so, a girl with psychic abilities would surely have been remembered," I said. "Your account of desks moving around the room and so on is not the sort of thing people are inclined to forget."

He folded his arms and shifted his weight from one foot to another. "No. That is quite remarkable, as you say."

"Then I wonder why no one remembers her," commented James.

"You'd have to ask them that, not me."

"Is it possible that you invented the story because it sounded more interesting for a stage performance?" I asked.

"A performance doesn't necessarily have to reflect real life, does it, Mrs Blakely? Some facts need to be altered to cater for the audience's particular tastes."

"By which you mean that you invented the story?"

"No, I stand by it. In fact, you can ask Miss Shelley yourself."

I turned to the young woman, who nodded meekly. It did not convince me at all, but I couldn't see what use there was in pursuing it further. Until I could prove that the professor was lying, there was nothing to gain by simply accusing him of it.

"Are we finished now?" asked Mrs Mortimer.

"Yes we are," said the professor. He turned to address James directly. "We've done what we can to assist you, Inspector. The spirit of Jane Bunton imparted as much as she wished to. I had hoped we would uncover the murderer this evening, but sadly that wasn't to be."

James put his notebook away. "I'll need to speak to the three of you again," he said.

"Of course, Inspector." The professor gave an obsequious bow, but there was a hard glint in his eye.

James and I stepped out of the dressing room and into the corridor. I was just about to comment on the professor's devious character when three men strode into view wearing dark clothing, flat caps and collarless shirts. My instinct was to shrink away from them.

As they passed us, one of them studied James, as if he recognised that he was a detective. We turned to watch them stop at the dressing room door behind us.

"Who are they?" I whispered.

"I don't know. Professor Mortimer obviously keeps interesting company."

CHAPTER 26

A letter from my father arrived the following morning. I opened it at the breakfast table.

Dearest Penny and James

I write to you in the hope that you will share my delight in response to recent news from Amazonia. Malia's sister, Juliana, is to marry the son of a prominent tribal leader. Malia, as you can imagine, is extremely happy about this news and would very much like to attend the celebrations. This means we will be setting sail a week from now.

We are also looking forward to your visit with great anticipation, of course. However, in light of this news from Colombia, we would appreciate it if you could bring your planned visit forward a little. Wednesday 21st would suit us extremely well. I trust this won't cause you any great inconvenience.

With my very fondest regards,
Father

"Wednesday?!" I exclaimed.

"What's happening on Wednesday?" asked James.

I showed him the letter.

"He always wants everybody to fit in with his plans," I said. "Never mind that we have our own lives here in London to attend to."

"It will be quite impossible for me to travel to Liverpool next Wednesday. That's only five days away! I can't even consider it until we've caught Jane Bunton's murderer."

"I don't want to go without you."

"I'm afraid you'll have to on this occasion."

"Why does he have to go to Colombia? Why can't Malia travel on her own?"

"It's understandable that he would want to accompany her. She is his wife."

"*Common-law* wife."

"And the mother of his children. Presumably they'll be travelling, too."

I sighed and sat back in my chair. "Wednesday is no good."

"You have work to do as well, I suppose."

"Well, I did. But now that Mr Sherman has left the *Morning Express,* I presume the newspaper will no longer be requiring my services."

"Are you quite sure of that?"

"Oh, I don't know. But I know that I don't want to write anything for Crispin Childers. He's a dreadful man."

"If Wednesday isn't suitable, you must write to your father and tell him that."

"But then I won't be able to see him or meet his family until... who knows when?"

"He'll come back, won't he?"

"I imagine so. Or maybe he won't. After all, he was perfectly happy there for ten years." I took a sip of tea. "I'll pay Eliza a visit to find out what she thinks."

"I received a similar letter this morning," my sister confirmed when I arrived at her home in Bayswater.

"He expects us to just drop everything and rush straight up to Liverpool!"

"Is that not practicable for you?"

"No, it isn't. And it's especially impracticable for James. He can't just take a break from his job whenever he chooses. This sort of thing needs to be agreed with his employer in advance. It's so typical of Father. He only ever thinks of himself!"

"I agree, he does. But the wedding is an important event for his family, Penelope."

"It certainly seems that way." I sank onto the settee. "Perhaps there's no need for us to meet them after all."

"Oh, but I should like to meet them."

"So should I, but I can't just rearrange everything to suit him."

"I don't see what the problem is. We can just reschedule the train tickets and the hotel booking."

"But I have things to do here." Although I was probably no longer needed at the *Morning Express*, I wanted to do whatever I could to help with the Jane Bunton case. "I don't see why he couldn't bring his family down here for a day or so."

"Maybe you could suggest that to him."

"Perhaps I could. I'll ask Mrs Garnett what she thinks." I knew that my former landlady also wanted to visit Father and his family.

Eliza's maid brought in a coffee pot and two cups on a tray, setting them down on a low table. Eliza thanked her and requested that the door be closed behind her as she left.

"Francis quite surprised me during our stroll yesterday," she said as she poured out the coffee.

"Really?"

"Yes, his conversation took rather a different turn from usual. He said he'd been thinking about the future."

"Oh?"

"He's thirty-four now. Old enough to decide on his future path, yet he seems quite undecided." Her voice wavered a little, as if she felt some sadness as she recalled the conversation. "He enjoys his work at the library," she continued, handing me a cup of coffee, "but he doesn't want to work there forever."

"What else does he envision for the future?"

"Well, that's about it. He mentioned his love of travel again. It seems the travel bug really bit him when he journeyed to South America to find Father."

"How do you feel about travelling?"

"I've already explained that I have no desire to leave my children behind."

"They have a nanny. And George."

"I realise that. But to be frank with you, Penelope, I don't really relish the idea of travelling. I haven't inherited Father's love of adventure. In fact, it was probably his love of adventure, coupled with his prolonged absence from home, that has set my mind quite against the idea. What's the point? I'm quite happy here."

"So there was no talk of—"

"Marriage? None." She sat down with her cup of coffee and blew on it.

"Perhaps he's working himself up to it. Maybe yesterday's conversation was just an initial discussion, and he was trying to find the courage to propose. Perhaps he planned to do so, but was too nervous to go through with it and spent the time talking about other things instead. I can imagine him doing that."

"Perhaps you can. But the long and the short of it is that

marriage was never mentioned. I think if he truly wished to marry me, he would have mentioned it by now."

"But we're talking about Francis! He's a reserved English gentleman, and he takes his time about things. I wouldn't be disconsolate if I were you, Ellie. I'm sure he just needs to be completely ready before he can bring himself to mention it."

"I think it is rather curious that he brought the future up all of a sudden when he'd never mentioned it before."

"Perhaps he'd been mulling it over and finally felt ready to broach the topic."

"Or perhaps someone suggested it to him." She held my gaze.

"Perhaps someone did. Or perhaps he thought of it himself."

"I was wondering if you had mentioned it to him, Penelope."

I wanted to deny it, but I detected warmth in my face. My sister always knew when I was lying.

"I didn't ask him to discuss it with you," I said. "I merely made a general enquiry around—"

"You decided to make an intervention."

"No! I didn't intervene at all. Francis and I were talking in quite general terms, and then the conversation turned to you. I simply asked him if he considered the future at all."

"And that's why he brought it up with me."

Eliza seemed disappointed that he hadn't raised the topic of his own volition. I realised it wasn't ideal that he had only discussed it with her because I had mentioned it to him a few days previously.

"Anyway, I don't wish to dwell on it too much, as I've had a lot to consider. It's been a dreadful week, Penelope. Miss Barrington is currently reviewing my position."

"Oh no! Did she find out about your donation to Mrs Reddings?"

"She did indeed. And my donation to the other tenant."

"You gave her money, too?"

"What else was I supposed to do? These families are desperate."

"How did Miss Barrington find out about it?"

"A third tenant told her. A woman who, I should add, approached me when she heard about the two donations I'd made and wanted some money for herself. I felt her conditions weren't as desperate."

"And you refused her?"

"Yes, and that caused no end of trouble. The very first thing she did was report me to Miss Barrington. She didn't tell her she'd asked me for money, by the way; she merely told my employer about the other donations I had made."

"And what did Miss Barrington say about it?"

"She was extremely disappointed. Apparently, I've broken the trust in our relationship. Rather an exaggeration, if you ask me, but then Miss Barrington tends to be rather dramatic."

"I suppose she's angry that you broke the rules."

"Thank you for reminding me, Penelope."

"But you only broke the rules because you care, Ellie."

Her frown lifted a little. "Well, that is true. I didn't do anything malicious, did I?"

"Do you think she'll allow you to keep your position?"

"I don't know. She was quite angry with me. She kept talking about loyalty and trust, and I suppose those are the values that matter to her the most. I apologised profusely and assured her that there would be no repeat, but I shall just have to wait and see. How I wish now that I hadn't given in! But it's extremely difficult to stand by and watch young children suffer when you know you could do something to help."

"Perhaps this isn't the best line of work for you, Ellie," I cautiously suggested. "Even if Miss Barrington allows you to keep your job, there will be many other families in dire circumstances who will tug at your heartstrings."

"Yes, I suppose there will be."

"It's a very honourable occupation," I continued, "and whoever does it needs to be kind-hearted. But he or she also needs to be hardened to the task. It's possible to be too kind-hearted."

Eliza pondered this. "I can agree with that, and perhaps my nerves are a little too delicate. One's nerves suffer terribly after one becomes a mother. Until that point, one can maintain an element of hardness, as you put it, but once you have children of your own and see other children suffering..." Her eyes grew damp. "Perhaps I overestimated my ability to do the job. I'm no good at it..." She pulled out a handkerchief and dabbed at her face.

I leaned forward and rested my hand on her knee. "I'm sure you're very good at it, Ellie. Perhaps it's best to wait and see what Miss Barrington says. If she wants you to stay, I think you should. I'm sure you'll find it difficult at times, but the tenants would miss having you there to help them. You probably shouldn't give them your money, but you can help in many other ways."

CHAPTER 27

I travelled from Bayswater to Moorgate by underground railway. The fifteen-minute journey gave me time to ponder the predicament of visiting my father. *Was I foolish in thinking I still needed to work on the Jane Bunton case? If I was no longer working in my capacity as a news reporter, what was my role to be?* I could assist James, as I had with many cases in the past, but it seemed rather amateurish to assist him merely because I was his wife. And it would be difficult to speak to people without being able to say that I was reporting for the *Morning Express*.

Although I had officially left the newspaper several months previously, Mr Sherman had continued to provide me with a regular source of work. I had written for various other publications as well, but most of that work had been limited to the subjects women were traditionally permitted to write about, such as the latest fashions and tips for running a household.

With few pressing demands on my time, there was no reason why I shouldn't visit my father on the date he had suggested. But I didn't like the thought of leaving James behind in London. I knew he would manage perfectly well without me, but I feared missing out on an important development in the investigation. And besides, I felt that I was familiar enough with the facts of the case to be useful.

I turned right after leaving Moorgate station, then right again along Fore Street. This was a familiar route from the days when this place had been my home. I was less accustomed to the noise and bustle now, and it was difficult to believe that the sound of the trains passing in and out of Moorgate had so often lulled me to sleep at my former lodgings.

On reaching Milton Street, my eye was drawn to a sign outside Mrs Garnett's townhouse. I felt a twinge of sadness as I noticed the word 'Sold' painted across it. I walked up the street and rang the bell.

"My last tenant moved out on Friday," explained Mrs Garnett as she led me into her parlour, "and I shall hand the keys over to the new owner this coming Friday." She glanced around her. "It's the end of an era."

"It certainly is." My throat tightened.

I had never felt any great affection for Mrs Garnett in the past. At times when I had been short of money and struggled to pay my rent, she had seemed quite uncaring. But having seen the kindness she extended to my father during his tenancy here, I had discovered a newfound fondness for her. Besides this, she seemed frailer than she had been the last time I saw her, and somehow less intimidating. The thought of her moving away saddened me.

"Do you think you'll ever come back to visit the house?" I asked.

She sucked the air in through her teeth. "No. It's never a good idea to return to the past, Mrs Blakely. I'd prefer to remember this place the way it is now. The new owner will come along and change everything, so there's no use in me coming back to visit."

She invited me to take one last look at my former room. We climbed the broad, carpeted staircase, followed by the narrow wooden staircase that led up to the garret room at the top of the house.

As we stepped inside, a ray of sunshine streamed in through the window where my writing desk had once stood. The room was empty now. I glanced over to where my bed and wardrobe had been, and then at the little stove at the far end of the room. I walked over to the window and looked out at the view. I had procrastinated for many hours in this spot, watching the ever-changing sky over the rooftops. Tiger had prowled about on the small area of flat roof below, stalking pigeons and bathing in the sunshine whenever the weather allowed it.

I turned back to face the room, which seemed much smaller with its bare floorboards and lack of furniture. I understood why Mrs Garnett preferred not to return to the past. Empty and devoid of any soul, this room was not how I wanted to remember it. I felt as if I were looking into the lifeless face of a dearly departed friend.

Tears prickled my eyes. "Thank you, Mrs Garnett. I've seen enough now. Like you, I'd prefer to remember this place as it was."

I saw that her eyes were also damp. "It was a pleasure to have you as a tenant here, Mrs Blakely."

"Even when I couldn't pay my rent on time?"

She laughed and laid an affectionate hand on my shoulder. "Yes, despite that. And you always paid eventually, didn't you? You were a good tenant, and I shall miss you."

She leaned in and embraced me. She was no longer my landlady; instead, she felt like an elderly aunt.

"What will you do when you move out to the country?" I asked as we walked back down the stairs.

"My sister has a smallholding, so I shall help her with that. She's older than me and needs some assistance, and I think I'll enjoy having some time to sew and read. I'm hoping it'll be a much quieter life. You're very welcome to visit any time you like. It's only a two-hour journey from Waterloo."

We stepped into her parlour and Mrs Garnett offered me a glass of coca wine. "It's the last bottle your father brought me."

"Oh, all right." I usually refused it, but this time I relented.

"Talking of your father, I received a letter from him this morning asking me to go and see him next Wednesday. He's heading back to Amazonia."

"Yes, that was something I wanted to discuss with you."

"I shall enjoy the trip. Are you looking forward to it?"

"I am, but next week isn't very convenient."

"Why not?"

"James won't be able to come."

"You could go without him. You don't have to spend all your time with your husband, you know."

"I realise that."

"You must see your father before he makes that long journey again. You never know when you'll next get the opportunity."

"No, but—"

"Never underestimate the importance of family, Mrs Blakely."

CHAPTER 28

James and I met inside the Museum Tavern. We sat at a table that was partitioned either side with wooden screens. Carved glass mirrors reflected the flickering gas lights, and the air was heavy with pipe smoke.

"We arrested Professor Mortimer, Mrs Mortimer, and Miss Shelley today," he announced.

"Do you think they're all responsible for Jane Bunton's murder?"

"The only evidence we have so far is the description we were given by Samuel Bunton. But I wasn't at all convinced by the professor's manner when we spoke to him yesterday evening. I sensed he was trying to hide something from us. I visited the doctor who provided him with an alibi."

"Dr Corkhill?"

"That's the one. A pleasant chap, but completely unreliable, just as you suggested. When I challenged him about the date and time of their meeting, he became quite confused and flustered. It's safe to say that Professor Mortimer's alibi is not a solid one. The same goes for Miss Shelley. Her alibi was provided by Mrs Mortimer, and one could argue that Mrs

Mortimer has a vested interest in covering for the young woman. My plan is to question Miss Shelley without her guardians present. It's impossible to get a straight answer from her while they're around."

"You must be careful with her, James. She's only young."

"She's old enough to know what she's doing."

"Yes, but I suspect the Mortimers have managed to exert a great deal of control over her."

"I can't understand why you have so much sympathy for her, Penny."

"She's only fifteen."

"Young people can still be involved in murder."

"I realise that, but she probably feels it would be impossible to stand up to Professor Mortimer and his wife. I suspect the story of the workhouse waif isn't true, which means there's something he's hiding. I think she's frightened of him, and that means she'd probably do anything he asked of her."

"Let's assume for a moment that she is frightened of him," replied James. "Even so, the young woman would have stood up to him if there had been any mention of murder. She cannot completely absolve herself of responsibility if she didn't. She could have run off to the police station and reported them."

"Perhaps she was too frightened."

"Nonsense! She couldn't possibly have been too frightened to report a murder plot. It would have been common sense to find the nearest police station as soon as she heard of the plan and reveal what was happening. They would have protected her and arrested the Mortimers. I'm sorry, Penny, but I think you have extended far too much compassion toward Miss Shelley. You have to accept that, despite her youth, she is quite capable of doing something as unpleasant as this without being coerced.

"And let's not forget that her supposed powers are far from genuine. She spends most evenings on stage pretending she can communicate with the spirits. That's a perfect example of her dishonesty right there. She may be young, but she's perfectly willing to pull the wool over people's eyes. She has already demonstrated that she can manipulate people and make them believe in a fantasy world. I think you're being taken in by her, Penny, even if she does look young and innocent. There's a strong chance that she's every bit as guilty as Professor Mortimer and his wife."

I took a sip of sherry. Frustratingly, there was a strong possibility that James was correct. I had sensed an air of vulnerability in Miss Shelley's manner. There was something about her large, pleading eyes that made me believe she was innocent. But until I could find any evidence that she was, there was no use in me trying to persuade James otherwise. As far as he was concerned, he had arrested his chief suspects and was making progress with the case. I had to prove somehow that Miss Shelley shouldn't be charged. And it wasn't going to be easy.

CHAPTER 29

A telegram arrived for me the following day, and I was surprised to discover that it was from Edgar Fish. It informed me that a visitor had arrived to see me and requested that I travel to the *Morning Express* offices at my earliest convenience.

I arrived there an hour later and found Edgar and Frederick Potter chatting in the newsroom.

"I thought you'd both decided to leave the paper," I said.

"We had," responded Edgar, whose feet were resting up on the desk.

"We both had," added Frederick.

"But then Mr Conway had a word with us," continued Edgar, "and he discussed a revised remuneration with us."

"He offered you a better wage?" I asked.

"That's about the long and the short of it, yes."

"But I thought you couldn't bear to work here without Mr Sherman?"

"We didn't want to, but we've had a few days of Childers now, haven't we, Potter? And he isn't all that bad."

"I distinctly recall you saying that you detested him."

"We did, didn't we, Potter? But a chap can change his mind."

"You mean to say that the extra money changed your mind?"

"There's nothing wrong with that, Mrs Blakely. This job is our bread and butter. Anyway, you have a visitor."

"Who is it?"

"She went off for a little walk, but she should be back shortly."

"She?"

"What did she say her name was again, Potter?"

"Jones, I think she said."

"Edith Jones?" I asked.

"Could be."

"In that case, it's Jane Bunton's housekeeper."

"She came here because she wanted to speak with you and wasn't sure where else to find you."

"I wonder what she wanted to speak to me about."

The newsroom door opened and a pale, narrow-faced man stepped into the room. His hair was so fair that it was almost white.

His eyes rested on me. "Oh, good morning," he said. "I thought you'd left."

I heard Edgar suppress a snigger at the new editor's complete lack of manners.

"Good morning, Mr Childers," I replied. "It's a pleasure to meet you again. I think you knew me as Miss Green when we last met. I'm Mrs Blakely now. I left the *Morning Express* when I married, but I worked for Mr Sherman on an ad hoc basis after that."

He responded with an insipid smile. "And how can we help you?"

I explained that I had come to meet a visitor.

"But was I right in saying that you no longer work for the newspaper?"

"Yes."

"Well, then, I don't think I can agree to our offices being used as a meeting place for former employees."

"I'm sure you can't, and I wouldn't expect you to. The visitor, whose name, I believe, is Miss Jones, called here asking for me. I don't think she was aware that I no longer work here."

There was a polite knock at the newsroom door and Mr Childers answered it. Miss Jones stepped into the room wearing a black overcoat, her red hair pinned up beneath a black hat.

I greeted her.

"You can't just come barging in here, arranging to meet people, you know," Mr Childers said to her.

I heard Edgar snigger again.

"Thank you, Mr Childers," I said. "Miss Jones and I will be on our way now. It was nice to see you, sir, and good luck with the circulation figures. I know your uncle likes to keep a close eye on those."

I led the way down the stairs and out onto Fleet Street.

"I hope I haven't inconvenienced you," said Miss Jones. "It certainly seems as if I inconvenienced that gentleman."

"Oh, you mustn't worry about him. He's thoroughly miserable to everyone. Shall we take a walk by the river?"

"That would do nicely."

We crossed the road and turned left into Bouverie Street. The day had been sunny first thing, but large grey clouds were moving in on a chilly wind. Specks of rain began to land on my spectacle lenses.

"I'm so sorry to trouble you," said Miss Jones, "but I felt

the need to talk to someone about what's happened. I hear the young medium has been arrested. Is that right?"

"Yes, Miss Shelley has been apprehended, along with Professor and Mrs Mortimer."

"Will they all stand trial?"

"That hasn't been determined yet. More evidence needs to be found before they can be charged, but hopefully that will happen sooner rather than later."

"You mean they could be released again?"

"Yes, it's possible. Sometimes a little patience is required in cases like this, and that can be difficult. I've been involved with similar cases in the past, and there were times when it felt as if no progress were being made at all. But we persevered and got there in the end."

As I spoke, I was mindful of the fact that Miss Jones had no alibi for the time of Mrs Bunton's murder. *Might she have been capable of murdering her friend and employer?* I couldn't imagine it.

"I understand that my husband, Detective Inspector James Blakely, spoke to you," I said.

"Yes, and I've told him the same facts several times now. It seems I have to keep repeating myself."

This was a tactic James used to establish whether a suspect's story remained consistent, but I chose not to explain that to her.

"No one enjoys being questioned by the police," I said, "but it's essential that every avenue is investigated in a case like this. Sometimes the smallest clue can be the key to solving a murder."

"I'm rather worried that your husband thinks I had a motive for harming Jane."

"Such as?" I said, pretending he hadn't discussed it with me.

She cleared her throat. "Jane lent me a significant sum of

money, which I needed to support my mother. I hadn't asked to borrow it, but she knew my mother was experiencing financial difficulties and kindly offered it. I initially refused. 'Neither a borrower nor a lender be,' as Shakespeare said, 'for loan oft loses both itself and friend.'"

"Wise words."

"But my mother really needed some assistance, and I had grown quite desperate, so I accepted Jane's kind offer."

"Did you agree to any repayment terms?"

"We agreed that I would pay her a small amount each month once my mother's situation was resolved."

"And has it been resolved?"

"Unfortunately, it hasn't, and a further situation has truly complicated matters."

Her explanation was vague, and I wondered what the situation might be, but I had no wish to pry. On the other hand, her nebulous explanation might have been intentional because she had something to hide.

"Is the money you owed Mrs Bunton still outstanding?"

"Yes, it is."

"How did she feel about that?"

"I don't know. After she had lent me the money, she never mentioned it again."

"She didn't ask when you intended to repay it?"

"No."

We reached the Victoria Embankment and crossed the road to the riverside. A coal barge steamed slowly past as we made our way west toward Temple Pier.

"Am I right in thinking the only evidence to suggest that Miss Shelley and Professor Mortimer carried out the crime is reliant on Mr Bunton's word?" she asked.

"I can't say that for certain, but it was Mr Bunton's description of the assailants that caused them to be named as suspects early on in the investigation."

"And there were no other witnesses?"

"I don't know." Miss Jones was probably correct about this, but I didn't want to tell her too much about the investigation. As a suspect, she could use the information to her advantage if the need arose.

"If the only witness was Mr Bunton, he may simply have concocted the story," she commented.

I turned to face her. "When we last spoke, you said that you didn't want to talk about your employer."

"One or two things have happened since then that have caused me to change my mind."

"Such as?"

"Such as his friendship with Mrs Hargreaves. They seem to be spending a lot of time together."

"I recall speaking to Mrs Hargreaves. She's the neighbour who came to help Mrs Bunton that night, isn't she?"

"That's right. She and her husband were on friendly terms with Mr and Mrs Bunton. I'm not sure what her husband makes of her visiting the Bunton house so regularly! I know that his work as a lawyer keeps him busy, so perhaps he hasn't noticed."

"Are you suspicious of Mr Bunton's friendship with Mrs Hargreaves?"

"More than suspicious. I know for a fact that their relationship is not an appropriate one. I saw them locked in a tender embrace."

"Really? But Mr Bunton has only just been widowed. Are you certain you weren't mistaken?"

"Quite certain. The door to the drawing room has a habit of releasing itself from its latch. It's a repair I've been meaning to address for a little while. When the door slips its latch, it sits open by about half an inch. I happened to catch sight of them one day while I was passing."

It sounded to me as though she had been purposefully

peering in through the gap. Perhaps that was why she had been so slow to fix the door; the fault gave her the perfect opportunity to spy on her employers. This wasn't an unusual trait in servants. In this case, however, it seemed her nosiness might prove useful to the investigation.

"This affection they hold for each other," I began. "Do you know if it existed prior to Mrs Bunton's death?"

"Yes, I believe it did. They were certainly more discreet when Jane was alive, but I've been reappraising the interactions I recall seeing between them, and it seems quite obvious to me now that an affair had been taking place for some time."

"Do you think Mrs Bunton knew about it?"

"I doubt it, but I can't be sure of that. I think she would have mentioned it to me if she'd known."

"Was she happy in her marriage?"

"No, she wasn't. Forgive me for keeping this from you when we last spoke – I felt I should safeguard her secrets at the time. But I realise now that the affair may have had something to do with her death. Perhaps Mr Bunton murdered her so he could enjoy a full-blown love affair with Mrs Hargreaves. In which case, he may be lying about the people who supposedly attacked her."

"If that's the case, surely Mr Hargreaves is also an obstacle to the continuation of their affair?"

"Maybe Mrs Hargreaves is planning to get rid of him somehow? Or perhaps he's conducting an affair of his own and cares little for what his wife does? They're all dreadful people. I don't understand how anyone could behave as they are so soon after Jane's death! Don't they care for her memory at all? She would've been devastated if she'd seen what was happening." She shook her head, then dabbed at her eyes.

"Do you think Mr Bunton might have murdered his wife?" I asked.

She shrugged. "I never thought he'd be capable of such an act, but now I've seen how he is with Mrs Hargreaves I'm not so sure. The man clearly has a heart of stone!"

"He may be heartless, but does that make him a murderer?"

"I certainly think he's capable of it. If he was keen to be with his mistress, he could quite easily have shot his wife and pretended someone else had done it."

"Thank you for imparting this information to me today, Miss Jones. I think you need to go and tell it to the police now."

"But he might come after me if I do that!"

"Mr Bunton need never know that it was you who told them."

"But it'll be obvious."

"Does he know that you saw them through the gap in the door?"

"No."

"Then he doesn't even know you're aware of the affair. How could he suspect you? You must be brave, Miss Jones, and tell the police what you've just told me. Then they can speak to him, and even arrest him if they deem it necessary."

"I really don't want to."

"Why not?"

"I'd much rather you did it instead." She turned to me, her eyes pleading. "Please, Mrs Blakely. Will you do it?"

CHAPTER 30

Miss Jones and I took our leave of each other, and I continued my walk along the river to Scotland Yard. James had just returned to his office after spending the morning at Camden Town police station.

"I can't get a straight answer from that infernal professor," he fumed. "He's one of those chaps who just thinks he's cleverer than everyone else."

"Well, he is a professor, so I suppose he's probably cleverer than most people."

"Yes, when it comes to... what was it? Crystallisation, I think he said, and discovering new elements for that table, whatever that is."

"Periodic table. Did Dr Corkhill bore you with that?"

"Yes, he did. As I understand it, Mortimer failed to find a new element, so he can't be all that good. Anyway, he's been excelling himself in the art of obfuscation."

"Now *you* sound like a professor, James."

"He refused to give me any straight answers. Does that sound more fitting for a policeman?"

I smiled. "Yes, it does. I'm sorry to hear that Professor

Mortimer isn't being helpful; he's clearly hiding something. Did you speak to Miss Shelley?"

"Yes, and that was even worse! She gives nothing away at all. The girl barely speaks. What's a chap to do to get some words out of her? I threatened her with a week's imprisonment for lack of compliance, but even that wasn't enough to encourage her to talk."

"You threatened to imprison her? She's only fifteen, James!"

"That's old enough to cooperate with the police, I say. Anyway, she hasn't been imprisoned just yet. I left her with the inspectors from E Division to see whether they manage to get anywhere. I'll return at the end of the day to find out how they're getting on."

"You might want to speak to Samuel Bunton again, too," I said, summarising what Edith Jones had related to me.

"Why didn't she tell me that when I saw her last?"

"I don't know. It seemed as though she'd been mulling it over."

"It could be a strategic move on her part. If she murdered Mrs Bunton because they had fallen out over money, it would suit her to point the finger at Samuel Bunton."

"Very true. And for some reason she didn't want to speak to the police directly. Instead, she asked me to pass the information on."

"Lucky you, Penny. I don't understand why she's pulling you into all this, but I shall treat her story with the pinch of salt it probably deserves."

A constable interrupted us. "Your presence is required in Dulwich Village, sir. A suspected poisoning."

"Oh, dear. Dulwich, did you say?" He turned to me. "You were over that way recently, weren't you, Penny?"

I nodded.

James turned back to the constable. "Do you have any details about the victim?"

"An elderly gentleman," he replied, "residing at Farley Lodge."

"It's not Jeremiah Wigmore, is it?" I asked.

The constable's jaw dropped. "Yes, I believe that's his name, ma'am."

"It's Jane Bunton's father," I said. "Can I come with you, James?"

Within an hour we were standing in the large hallway of Farley Lodge listening to a briefing from Inspector Bridges of P Division. He was a red-cheeked man with a fleshy nose and a barrel-shaped chest.

"Mr Wigmore fell seriously ill yesterday evening and died shortly after being taken to his bedchamber," he explained. "The doctor was summoned and nothing initially appeared suspicious about the circumstances, especially as Mr Wigmore was a man of advanced age. However, the doctor grew curious when he detected the faint odour of bitter almonds."

"Cyanide," commented James.

"Exactly. The police surgeon has just completed a post-mortem and we're awaiting scientific analysis of various samples." He gave me a cautious glance before adding, "Stomach contents and the like. That's merely routine, of course, but it'll be important in a court of law. The police surgeon agrees with the doctor that the old man was poisoned. We're conducting a thorough search of the premises and stumbled upon several packets of rat poison. They may or may not have been used in the poisoning. It's a big place, so our search will continue for a while longer."

James glanced around the hallway. "It certainly is big."

"My men have been speaking with all the servants,"

continued Inspector Bridges. "Of particular interest to us, of course, is the cook, seeing as it's most likely that Mr Wigmore consumed the cyanide in his food. Unsurprisingly, the cook is extremely distressed by this tragic event, as are the other members of staff."

"When did he eat his last meal?" asked James.

"He consumed a beef pie at seven o'clock yesterday evening. He also drank three glasses of red wine and ate a raisin pudding. The remnants from the meal have been sent off for scientific analysis, as have various bowls, plates, cups and pieces of cutlery."

"Did he dine alone?"

"No, his daughter was with him."

"Mrs Harding?" I asked.

"Yes. Do you know her?"

"I've met her a couple of times."

"She's still here at the house and has been since her father's death. She's terribly distraught about it. The staff tell me she's inconsolable. It's been a dreadful time for the family, with Mr Wigmore having lost his other daughter just recently. Mrs Harding is the only family member who remains."

"Did Mrs Harding help prepare his food?" asked James.

"No, she didn't," Inspector Bridges replied. "She sat at the table with her father, however, and it could be argued that she had the opportunity to put the poison in his food while he was dining. But I can't see why she would have done such a thing. She and her father were already coping with a bereavement. Why would she want to poison him?"

"I suspect that, as his only surviving offspring, she stood to inherit his estate, and might also receive a life insurance sum," James replied.

"But he was already in such poor health," I said. "Why would she want to hasten his end?"

"It's very puzzling indeed," said James. "Have you interviewed her yet?"

"I attempted to," the inspector replied, "but the poor woman is distressed to the point of being unable to speak. She's currently resting in her bedchamber. I'm hoping she'll be in a fitter condition to speak to me a little later."

"Was Mrs Harding the only person Mr Wigmore dined with yesterday evening?" James asked.

"Yes."

"Who else was in the house?"

"Just the servants. I've interviewed them all, and everyone seems genuinely upset by his unnatural death. I'll go back through them again at some point and see what I can glean from that. Our investigation has been concentrating on the servants who were in either the kitchen or the dining room. Who had access to that pie or pudding? Or to his drink? A fair few of them, it would seem, and I plan to question them all thoroughly in the coming days."

"But what motive would the servants have for murdering their employer?" queried James.

"A grudge, perhaps," suggested the inspector. "I've seen it before. We'll have to spend time delving into Mr Wigmore's affairs and conduct, although I must say that the chap appears to have led a quiet life in recent years. His poor health limited his ability to do much at all. Anyway, I expect you'd like to have a look around, Inspector Blakely. And you'll want to speak to the staff, of course. I'll introduce them to you. In the meantime..." The inspector glanced at me. He was clearly surprised to see that James had brought his wife to the house with him, but was too polite to comment on it directly. "Mrs Blakely, would it trouble you to wait in the drawing room for a little while?"

"Not at all."

Inspector Bridges led me there. "I'll ask one of the maids to bring you some tea, Mrs Blakely."

"There's no need if everyone's rather distracted," I said.

"I'm sure it won't be a problem. Leave it with me."

Once he had left the room, I made myself comfortable on a faded velvet settee. The furniture in the drawing room was sturdy and well made, but it looked a little shabby; as if it had been passed down through numerous generations.

I would rather have accompanied James while he interviewed the servants. I was intrigued to hear what they had to say. *Why would someone have wished to murder Mr Wigmore?* It made little sense that such a frail, elderly man should have been harmed in this way. I felt a tinge of regret that I had been unable to speak to him about his daughter's death.

The tea arrived, and I took a book of poems out of my bag to occupy me while I waited. I had only opened it to the first page when the door swung open and Caroline Harding swept in with Tiny under her arm.

"Mrs Blakely? It seems you're determined to follow me about!"

I got to my feet and offered her my condolences. "I accompanied my husband here," I explained.

"I see."

Her large frame sank into a chair, practically covering it with the black silk and tulle of her extravagant mourning dress. She dropped Tiny onto the floor, and the little dog trotted over to me and sniffed my skirts.

"I don't think I can bear it," wailed Caroline. "What has my life become?"

"The cause of your father's death must have come as quite a shock," I commented.

"Oh, it did! Cyanide? Who on earth would have wanted to poison him?"

"Are you certain that he consumed it in his meal yesterday evening?"

"Oh, absolutely, yes. The doctor informed me that death brought on by cyanide is extremely swift. Once he was taken ill, the end was already nigh. And what an awful death! It may have been swift, but he suffered terribly during that brief time. I can't understand how anyone would have wanted to inflict that upon him."

"How do you think the poison got into his food?"

She shrugged. "I have no idea, but it must have happened before it was brought up from the kitchen."

"Was it just the two of you who dined together?"

"Yes. I realise the finger could easily be pointed at me, but I can assure you that I would never have poisoned my dear father. Why would I do that?"

I shook my head to imply that I couldn't think of a single reason.

"He was so elderly and unwell," she continued. "He still enjoyed his food, though. It was his favourite meal last night, beef pie. I knew I would need to start worrying when he stopped enjoying his food. But then... Oh, I just can't understand how it happened. And to think that I could have been poisoned, too! It just doesn't bear thinking about."

"Someone was clearly targeting him rather than you," I said. I wondered for a moment whether she had been the intended target, and somehow the plates had accidentally been swapped around.

"You have tea," she stated, staring at the tray on the table next to the settee. "I'd like some as well."

I couldn't offer her some of mine, there was only one cup and saucer.

"Oh, everything is quite dreadful!" she continued. "First Jane and now my father. Who could possibly hate my family so much that they would want to murder them both? Your husband had better get to the bottom of this quickly, Mrs Blakely. People can't just go around carrying out such horrific acts and be allowed to get away with it! They must be caught. I won't rest until they're hanged!"

"Were there any other visitors here yesterday?" I asked.

"None. Father was no longer in the habit of receiving visitors."

"Did someone come to deliver something? Or to repair something?"

"I really don't know; the housekeeper sees to all that. Your husband will have to ask her about it."

"Did you often dine with your father here?"

"Not terribly often, but it's something I've been doing more regularly in recent months, as his health has declined. About once a week, I suppose."

"Did he usually dine alone when you weren't here?"

"Oh, absolutely, yes. Who else was there to dine with? This house was once filled with family, but everyone has either moved away or died now. Or been murdered, for that matter. Why hasn't anyone offered me any tea yet?"

As at our last meeting, I found Caroline's manner odd. She seemed more aggrieved for herself than for her father. *Was it possible that she had poisoned him?* If so, I couldn't understand why she would do so when he presumably hadn't had much longer to live. I wondered if she had an urgent need for money.

An alternative explanation was that Caroline was entirely blameless, in which case someone appeared to have some sort of vendetta against the family.

But who? And why?

CHAPTER 31

"The servants are ever so upset," said James as we travelled back to London town by train. "It's awfully puzzling, because everyone I spoke to seemed quite genuine about their grief."

"And what of Mrs Harding?"

"She doesn't seem quite so genuine, does she? I don't see how she would have poisoned her father, though. There was a servant waiting table in the room where they dined most of the time. There would have been very few opportunities for her to slip any poison into his food."

"Especially without him noticing."

"Exactly. That would be rather tricky to do, wouldn't it?"

"She could have distracted him, I suppose. Perhaps she pretended something had fallen onto the floor. Or maybe she even knocked something onto the floor."

"That's a possibility. Cyanide is a powder, though. She wouldn't have been able to mix it into his food in such a brief moment of distraction."

"Perhaps she put it into his wine."

"I'm beginning to suspect that's the most likely explanation. A powder could be dropped into a drink quite quickly and all trace of it would disappear once it was dissolved. With good sleight of hand, I'm sure that could be achieved. The scientific analysis of the crockery and cutlery should help us establish how the cyanide was administered."

"Presumably, it would have been easy to obtain."

"Yes, there was a recently opened packet of rat poison in the scullery."

"But wouldn't the staff have noticed if Mrs Harding had gone in there? I can't imagine she's the sort of woman who would spend much time in a scullery."

"I agree. However, a determined murderer always finds ways and means."

"Is Mr Wigmore's murder connected to the death of his daughter, do you think?"

"That's a good question, and I wish I had the answer to it, Penny. The likelihood of two family members being murdered by different assailants within a few days of each other is fairly slim. Therefore, I'm tempted to believe that there must be a connection. But what that connection might be remains a mystery at the moment."

"Do you think Caroline Harding might have murdered them both?"

"She could have done. She must have been quite desperate for money to murder two members of her own family so swiftly, though. A little investigation into her financial affairs would certainly help us ascertain whether she was struggling or not. Let's not forget that we also have a motive for Samuel Bunton now. An affair with Mrs Hargreaves could explain why he wanted to be rid of his wife. There's a lot to consider. I'm beginning to doubt that Professor Mortimer and Miss Shelley carried out the attack on Mrs Bunton."

"But what about the description of the murderers?"

"Imposters, perhaps, or a story Mr Bunton concocted."

"Perhaps Mr Bunton and Mrs Harding are in cahoots."

James gave an exasperated laugh. "That's another possibility for us to consider. This investigation is expanding all the time, isn't it? We'll need to question Mr Bunton and Mrs Harding in more detail."

"And Miss Jones."

"Yes, she's a funny one. For the time being, we'll have to release the Mortimers and Miss Shelley, and turn our attention to the other characters in this strange saga."

CHAPTER 32

Only four days remained until our departure for Liverpool. Discovering the truth about Jane Bunton's death within that time seemed an impossible task. The mystery surrounding Elizabeth Shelley's background still puzzled me, and I wondered if something useful might be achieved if I visited Camden Town again.

I recalled Miss Shelley's account about the eyes of the devil comment. The presence of the girl's mother in this story suggested it had happened before she met Professor Mortimer. Perhaps I could locate the church and find someone who remembered Miss Shelley as a child.

I made the journey to Camden Square once again, as I remembered seeing the tall spire of a church there. It was unlikely to be the church Miss Shelley had visited as a youngster, but I had to begin somewhere.

The spire of St Paul's Church was almost lost in fog by the time I arrived. The building was modern yet beautiful, with tall, arched, Gothic windows.

The vicar was leafing through notes at the lectern. He was a bald-headed man with thick-lensed spectacles and didn't

THE CAMDEN SPIRITUALIST

appear to relish my interruption. I introduced myself then related Miss Shelley's story to him. He listened impassively, giving little response as I spoke. I wasn't even halfway through my story before I gleaned that he had no recollection of it.

"I'm sorry, Mrs Blakely, but I don't think anything like that has ever happened here. Are you sure it was this church?"

"No, I can't be sure that it was here, but this is the closest church to the place where I believe she may have lived at the time."

"I don't remember anything like that at all. The nearest church to this one is St Luke's on Oseney Crescent. All I can suggest is that you try there."

"You don't remember ever meeting a young girl with psychic abilities?"

"Certainly not, and it isn't the sort of behaviour I would encourage. If any member of my congregation were afflicted in such a way, I would take great pains to resolve it."

"Would you perform an exorcism?"

"It would depend on the exact nature of the affliction, but yes, exorcism is one method of ridding people or places of unwanted spirits. In the case you mention, it's a sign that something has gone very wrong indeed. I do hope the young lady you mentioned decides to seek help and guidance from the church. The very worse course of action would be to treat an affliction of that sort as a form of entertainment. The girl needs deliverance and should certainly not be encouraged to make any form of communication with spirits. It can be exceptionally dangerous. Perhaps you could pass my message on to her when you next see her."

"Indeed, I will."

I followed the vicar's directions to St Luke's, and soon

reached a red-brick church surrounded by large, expensive-looking homes.

Inside, a bent, elderly woman in a grey woollen dress was wiping down the pews with a cloth. "The vicar isn't here at the moment," she said. "He's out and about, visiting his parishioners. He'll be here this afternoon if you'd like to come back then."

I told her my reason for visiting and related Miss Shelley's story in the hope that she might have heard it from someone else, if not first hand. But once again, my words were met with a blank expression.

"I'm sorry that I can't be of any help. Please do come back later. Four o'clock should probably do it."

I thanked her for her time and asked if there were any other churches in the area.

"You could try St Thomas's, down by the railway line."

I followed a route that took me back through Camden Square. From there I headed south, and as I did so the middle-class homes gave way to narrower streets lined with small, terraced houses. Children played on the cobbles, some of them barefoot. Stray dogs sniffed at the gutters and a man in dirty, under-sized clothes watched me as I passed, a thin clay pipe in his mouth. *Was it possible that Miss Shelley had grown up in an area as poor as this?*

St Thomas's was situated in the middle of a terraced street. Beyond a high wall at the end of the street came the whistle of a train.

I found the church empty, but discovered the sexton working out in the churchyard. He was a grey-haired man in a flat cap, with a waistcoat and rolled-up shirt sleeves. He listened with interest as I gave my reason for being there. I was already growing a little tired of the story and hoped I wouldn't have to repeat it many more times.

He listened intently and nodded repeatedly, which I took as an encouraging sign.

"Have you heard this story before?" I asked hopefully.

"Not that story, no. But I do remember the girl."

I felt a flip of excitement in my chest. "You do?"

"Yeah. It was when you was sayin' about them odd-coloured eyes. That's what I remember."

"Do you remember her name?"

"Nope. Can't tell you much more than that."

"Did she live here?"

"Yeah, somewhere round 'ere. I can't say as they came to this church, but lots o' people were talkin' about the girl with them odd eyes. Everyone thought it were a sign."

"A sign of what?"

"Well, that's where opinions was divided. Some thought as she were blessed, others thought as it were a curse. There was some what thought the devil had summink to do with it, like the woman you was just mentionin'. I would see 'er with 'er family on the 'igh street sometimes."

"What do you remember of her family?"

"Not a lot. There was a mother, as you'd expect. Don't remember seein' a father, mind you. And then there was little 'uns and a few big 'uns. Quite a lotta children, there was. She'd of been somewhere in the middle, age-wise."

"Do you remember the family name?"

"I might've known it once, but I couldn't tell you it now."

"Do you know anyone who might be able to?"

"Can't think of no one. I can ask around, if yer like. My wife would've known the name, but she's been dead and gone two years now."

"I'm sorry to hear it."

"Ain't your fault." He adjusted his cap. "Anyway, good luck findin' 'er." He returned to his work, making it abundantly clear that our conversation was over.

I called at several houses in the surrounding streets, hoping that someone else might recall the girl with mismatched eyes. It swiftly proved to be a fruitless task. Some were reluctant to speak to me at all, while others decided to relate tales that had no connection at all to my original question. A couple recalled seeing her, but, like the sexton, were unable to suggest a name or historical address.

Feeling unusually tired, I leaned against a wall to recover.

"Whatcha doin', lady?" asked a young boy with a grubby face.

"I'm looking for someone."

"Who?"

"Elizabeth Shelley. Do you know her?"

"Nope."

I tried not to become despondent. The fact that I had found a few people who remembered her was encouraging. It meant she must have grown up in the Camden area. It could only be a matter of time before I found someone who had known the family well.

Once I was suitably revived, I knocked on a few more doors.

"Brown," said a woman with a gaunt face and straw-like hair. Her arms were firmly folded over a worn shawl as she leaned against the door frame. "I fink that's what they was called. Brown, I'm sure of it. Didn't live on this street, though... fink they was over Priory Street way. Near the railway station."

"Can you remember the name of the girl?"

She squinted and gazed upward as she tried to remember. "Milly, was it? Or Molly? I reckon it were Milly 'cause I fink she were Millicent, but they was always callin' 'er Milly. That might of been 'er, or it might of been one o' the sisters. One of 'em was called Milly, I know that. I remember them eyes more'n anythin' else. Beautiful, they was."

"Can you remember how old she was?"

"Seven, maybe. Could of been older, 'cause she were quite small for 'er age. Possibly nine."

"Thank you."

I felt so relieved to have finally uncovered some useful information that I gave the woman a shilling.

I finally had a name. Millicent Brown. I began walking toward Priory Street, but another wave of fatigue gripped me. I paused for a moment to steady myself against a tree.

"Are you all right, madam?" asked a red-haired lady with a shopping basket.

"I'm fine, thank you. I'm just a little tired." I felt as though I were sickening for something. I hailed a cab to take me home.

CHAPTER 33

"It seems Professor Mortimer was lying about Elizabeth Shelley's background," said James after I had told him about my visit to Camden. "Just as you suspected."

"I'll go and speak to him about it tomorrow," I said. "It'll be interesting to hear how he responds."

"Not too favourably, I imagine. People never like to be found out. He might deny it all, and what proof do you have?"

"Perhaps Miss Shelley, or I should say Miss Brown, will tell me the truth."

"If she even remembers the life she had before her time with the Mortimers."

"She must do. She told me about that incident at the church, didn't she? And the woman I spoke to recalls her being between the ages of seven and nine. The Mortimers have tried to make her forget about her former life, I feel sure of it, but she must recall something."

"It makes sense to speak to them about it, and now that you're armed with the right information, it'll be difficult for them to deny."

"But even if they tell me the truth, I can't see how it will help us find Mrs Bunton's murderer."

"I suspect the answer lies within Jane's family. Her father's murder has to be connected, so that's where the investigation will need to be focused. My men have spent the day interviewing the servants at Farley Lodge, but nothing encouraging has emerged yet."

"What about Caroline Harding?"

"I think she has to be our prime suspect at this point in time."

A ring at the door interrupted us. Mrs Oliver answered it, then stepped into the front room to announce that Mr Bunton wanted a word with us.

"Samuel Bunton?" James got to his feet. "How on earth did he find out where I live?"

"The directory, I suppose," she responded.

James sighed. "Show him in, please, Mrs Oliver."

She had barely left the room when Samuel Bunton marched in. He was a tall man and seemed to take up a lot of space in our front room. I instinctively felt uncomfortable in his presence. His square jaw jutted out pugnaciously, and I saw a sharp glint in his small, dark eyes.

"What's this I hear about Mortimer being released?" Drops of spittle flew from his mouth as he spoke. "Why hasn't he been charged? No one else matches the description I gave you, yet you've let him and that strange witch-child go!"

"We're still considering the possibility that Professor Mortimer carried out the attack," said James. He stood smaller than Mr Bunton, but his stance was firm and his voice calm. "However, we need more evidence before we can charge him and put him on trial. I realise this must be extremely frustrating for you, Mr Bunton, but we need to make sure we have all the necessary evidence before we proceed. I'm sure you'd agree that it would be a mistake to press on with insufficient evidence and have Professor Mortimer and Miss Shelley acquitted as a result."

"What more do you need? I told you who shot my wife dead on my doorstep. I'll stand up in court as your chief witness and tell the judge and jury exactly what I saw!"

"There are other suspects we must also consider," replied James.

"Such as?"

"That's something I must keep confidential at the present time."

"But I'm Jane's husband! I have a right to know who you're considering as suspects in her murder!"

"We'll keep you informed as best we can—"

"But you're not keeping me informed at all! In fact, I've had to hire my own people to look into it."

"I would strongly advise against that course of action, Mr Bunton. You'd be better off leaving the investigation to the experts at Scotland Yard."

"That's what I've been doing all this time, and you've done nothing! In fact, it's even worse than that. You've gone and released the very people who murdered my wife!"

"You must allow us time, Mr Bunton. It's a complicated case and we're doing everything we can to solve it. We're working carefully and methodically. These things cannot be rushed."

"Clearly not. It's just been such a dreadful time. And now Jane's father is dead as well."

"Please accept my condolences."

"I've always held Scotland Yard in such high regard, but now I'm beginning to realise how incompetent you all are!"

"There's no need for insults, Mr Bunton."

"I say there's every need for them! Until decent progress is made, I shall have my own men working on the case."

"It'll only complicate matters. I must politely request that you ask them not to interfere. I don't want your men antagonising our witnesses and meddling with the investigative process."

"But whatever you've been doing isn't working. Am I wrong, Inspector? My men need to be involved if we're to get to the bottom of this."

James sighed and altered the course of the conversation. It was a tactful move to defuse the visitor's inflamed temper. "While you're here, Mr Bunton, there are a few things you can help me with."

"Like what?" He folded his arms.

"Can you describe your relationship with Mrs Bunton's sister, Caroline Harding?"

"There isn't any relationship between us. She's a selfish woman who walks around with a silly little dog and spouts nothing but nonsense all day long."

"When did you last see her?"

"She's called on me twice since Jane died. And duty will compel me to call on her in the near future to express my regrets with regard to her father."

"Did you know that Mr Wigmore was poisoned?"

"No!" His jaw dropped. "He was poisoned? How?"

"Cyanide was mixed into his food or drink. We're uncertain which it was yet, but we'll soon find out."

"But why would anyone want to do that?"

"I could ask you the same question, Mr Bunton."

"I have no idea. Who had the opportunity?"

"The household staff and Mrs Harding."

"Caroline was there? But she would never..." His eyes drifted across the room as he considered whether his sister-in-law could have poisoned her father. "It has to have been one of the staff," he added. Then he fixed James with his stony gaze again. "Professor Mortimer obviously paid someone to murder him!"

"But why would Professor Mortimer want Mr Wigmore dead?"

"Some sort of gruesome revenge, I would say. It has to be. He didn't like Jane, so he wanted her and her whole family to suffer."

"Maybe." The tone of James's voice suggested to me that he wasn't at all convinced. "What was your relationship with your father-in-law like?"

"I didn't poison him, if that's what you're suggesting." His chin jutted out again.

"I wasn't suggesting that at all. I'm simply trying to establish as much as I can about Mr Wigmore's life."

"He's pretty much been a recluse for the past year, as his health was so poor. He didn't go to many places other than church, and he didn't receive many visitors, either. I don't think he ever fully approved of me marrying Jane, but I don't suppose anyone would ever have been good enough for her as far as he was concerned."

"He was fond of her?"

"Exceptionally fond. He was devastated by her death."

"You mentioned that he never fully approved of you, Mr Bunton. How did that affect your relationship?"

"It didn't, really. He was an educated man with good manners. He treated me fairly, despite what he almost certainly thought about me privately. I respected him a great deal for that."

"And what of Mrs Hargreaves?"

A dramatic change came over Mr Bunton, as though he had been slapped across the face. "Pardon?"

"Your neighbour," continued James.

"What of her?"

"Would you say that you're on good terms with her?"

"I don't see what that has to do with anything."

"I'm just gathering information, Mr Bunton."

"You need to do more than gather information, Inspector. You need to charge Professor Mortimer and that witch-child right away and stick them on trial!"

"Perhaps you could describe the nature of your relationship with Mrs Hargreaves for me."

I didn't like the way Mr Bunton's face paled and his fists clenched in response to this. He took a breath, which I prayed would subdue any violent outburst.

"She and Mr Hargreaves are good friends of mine, and they were good friends to both Jane and myself while Jane was alive. If you've been listening to idle gossip, Inspector, I must advise you to rid your mind of it completely. This has nothing to do with Mrs Hargreaves, her husband or any other neighbour or acquaintance of mine, for that matter."

"Thank you for clarifying that."

Mr Bunton pointed his finger accusingly at James. "I can't help thinking that you're intent on barking up the wrong tree, Inspector. I have no confidence whatsoever in your abilities. Not only will I be informing your superiors of that, but I shall also ensure that my men investigate properly."

"That would be a very bad move," responded James.

There was no response. Mr Bunton had already left the room.

CHAPTER 34

I returned to Camden Square the following day and knocked at the well-polished door of Professor Mortimer's home.

The maid who answered appeared to recognise me from my previous visit. She probably assumed, as I had, that the professor would be happy to speak to me again. She returned a few minutes later, however, with a refusal.

"The professor and his wife have had a difficult few days and wish to be left in peace," she said.

"May I speak with Miss Shelley instead?"

"I'm afraid that won't be possible."

"Perhaps you could relay a message to Professor Mortimer from me," I said. "Would that be possible?"

The maid bit her lip as she considered this. "Very well."

"Could you please tell Professor Mortimer that I know who Millicent Brown is?"

"Millicent Brown?"

"Have you heard of her?"

She shook her head.

"I'd like to wait here in the hallway while you deliver that message, if that's all right. And then I'll be on my way."

She nodded and went off to speak to the professor again. She was gone longer than I had expected and I couldn't hear the conversation between her and the professor from my position in the hallway.

I thanked her when she returned and started making my way toward the front door.

"Mrs Blakely!" came a sharp voice from behind me.

"Yes, Professor?"

I turned and smiled at the familiar face standing in the doorway of the front room.

"What do you want?" he asked.

"Just a few minutes of your time," I responded. "And the truth."

I was shown into the front room, with its ornamental rug and paintings of classical buildings. The compilation of Greek tragedies still lay on the table, its cover and spine showing little sign of wear.

Professor Mortimer directed me to sit, but remained standing at the centre of the rug. "How did you find out about Millicent Brown?"

"Does the name mean anything to you?"

"I want to know where you heard the name before I embark on any sort of explanation."

"I discovered it during the course of my investigations here in Camden." I stared at him expectantly, hoping he would feel pushed into speaking honestly with me.

He stepped toward a chair, hitched his trousers up above the knee, and sat down. "You do realise the three of us were arrested the other day?" he asked me.

"Yes, so I heard."

"Your husband questioned us."

"He was just doing his job, Professor."

"Is that what you call it? My wife and Miss Shelley had to spend a night in the police cells! I can tolerate such treatment, but they shouldn't have to!"

"Are you going to tell me who Millicent Brown is?" I asked.

"I think you already know."

"I'd like to hear it from you."

"And *I* would like to hear what you know before I offer any further explanation."

I didn't want to tell him everything I knew. The information I possessed gave me a strong hand of cards, and with any luck, he would assume I knew more than I actually did. I decided to call his bluff and got to my feet. "I thought you were going to tell me the truth, Professor Mortimer," I said, "but if that's not the case, I shall be on my way. There's no point wasting any more of your time or mine."

"Wait." He clasped his eyes shut as he held out his hand. I knew he was reluctant to talk, but he seemed keen to find out what I knew. "Please sit, Mrs Blakely, and I shall tell you all about Millicent Brown. Perhaps I haven't been completely truthful about how I came to know Elizabeth Shelley, but you must understand that I only ever acted in her best interests."

He ran a hand over his wavy grey hair. "The Brown family was extremely poor. They were living on the very worst street in Camden Town. They had.... oh, I don't even know how many children. A lot! And Mrs Brown was struggling to adequately clothe and feed them. I couldn't tell you what had happened to Mr Brown. Perhaps he took to drink and lost his way home one night, never to be seen again. Who can tell?

"Anyway, I first saw Millicent in the marketplace. I should explain that I had already developed quite an interest in spiritualism by this time and was particularly fascinated by the case of the Fox sisters in America. Have you heard of them?"

I nodded.

"Kate and Margaretta. Many eminent men studied them, and opinions were divided whether their abilities were genuine or not. No matter what one's opinions are on the sisters, I think it speaks volumes that a good number of educated men considered it worth their while to study them."

"I see. You said that you saw Millicent at the market," I said.

"That's right. And from the moment I first laid eyes on her, I saw that she had a gift. I had once harboured an ambition to master psychic skills myself, but I realised it was a gift one is either born with or without. I knew instinctively that Millicent could do what I had always wanted to do."

"You were drawn to her unusual appearance?"

"Yes, to her mismatched eyes."

"How old was she?"

"About twelve. This will sound rather proud coming from me, Mrs Blakely, but the girl has undoubtedly enjoyed a superior quality of life than she otherwise would have had if she'd remained with her family. And her profession has allowed her to earn sums of money her family could only ever have dreamed of. What would have lain in store for her if she had remained with them? Probably servanthood before marriage, and a girl of her standing would not have married well. Money would always have been in short supply and life would have been difficult. Children would have been born, one after another, and all those extra mouths would have required feeding. One only has to look at the way the Brown family was living to know that it would have been just the same for Millicent. Poverty is a trap. There is no way out of it.

"I took it upon myself to take on this unusual girl and show her the extent of her powers," he continued. "Her mother didn't want me to, of course, which I suppose is a natural reaction for any mother. Why on earth would she want to hand her daughter over to a strange man? I visited the Brown household several times, but she refused to let me take her daughter. I explained that I wanted to give Millicent a good life and told her she could visit whenever she wished. Perhaps you also suspect my motives, Mrs Blakely. I took great pains to explain to Mrs Brown that I was a married man and did not have any ulterior motive, and yet she refused.

"All I could do was continue to meet with the girl – seemingly by accident, but really by design – and tell her about the life I could help her lead. It took a while to convince her, but she eventually agreed to come and live with me and my wife. I introduced her to Susanna, and we explained that we would give her an education and the sort of money her own family could never hope to provide. The girl was old enough to know her own mind, I would say.

"I visited the Brown family a few months later and explained that I would pay them a monthly stipend, asserting again that they could visit Millicent whenever they wished. I believe they alerted the police, but I must be frank and say that any policeman who visited the family home and saw the dire poverty would have realised the girl was enjoying a far better life here with me and Susanna. They chose not to investigate any further, and why would they? We had done a good thing. Millicent, or Elizabeth, as she is now called, would wholeheartedly agree."

"Why did you concoct the story about the workhouse waif?"

"Because it sounds far better in a theatre context. And it also served to protect the identity of her real family."

"Has Millicent ever expressed a wish to return to her family?"

"Elizabeth, you mean. No. No wish at all."

"Perhaps she could visit them now she's a bit older."

"There's no need! Elizabeth has all the fame and fortune she could ever wish for. Her mother has shown no pride, or even any interest, in her daughter's spiritual abilities, so the tie has been cut. I tried my hardest to appease the Browns, I really did." He wiped his brow, as though recalling the exertion of it all, "but the important thing is that the name Millicent Brown must remain a secret. It would not be fair on the family to have Elizabeth's true background revealed. I've stuck with the workhouse story all these years to protect people, and it must remain that way."

"Of course." I wanted him to think that I was cooperating, but I wished to ensure that her name became widely known. I felt eager to find Millicent's family so I could hear their side of the story.

The maid interrupted us. "Three visitors to see you, sir," she said.

"Again?"

She nodded.

The professor turned to face me. "I must see them, Mrs Blakely."

I thanked him for his time and made my way back to the hallway. I found the same three men standing there in flat caps and collarless shirts as I had seen in the corridor at the Theatre Royal. They stared as I passed, and I left the house as quickly as I could, the hairs prickling at the back of my neck.

CHAPTER 35

I travelled by omnibus to Trafalgar Square, then walked the short distance to Scotland Yard. I felt it was important that James knew Miss Shelley's full story as soon as possible.

I hoped Professor Mortimer had finally told me the truth. I wasn't enamoured by his depiction of himself as a saviour, however. While it seemed possible that Millicent Brown came from a poverty-stricken home, that didn't give him the right to take her from her family. And although she appeared to live in relative comfort now, it was possible she was being forced to perform as a medium against her wishes. The professor had admired the Fox sisters but I thought it unlikely that he would have been able to sense such abilities in a twelve-year-old he had encountered at a market. He had been keen to create a psychic sensation of his own and I suspected he had been drawn to Miss Brown's unusual appearance and hatched a plan to present her as a medium. To my mind, he was a fraud and Miss Brown was being exploited.

I hoped James would persuade one of his colleagues to help us find Millicent Brown's family in Camden.

"Penny! Is everything all right?" James was standing by his desk with a bunch of papers in his hand.

"Yes, but I thought you might be interested in hearing who Elizabeth Shelley really is. Or perhaps I should say Millicent Brown."

"Now?" He checked his pocket watch. "I'm just about to travel to Dulwich Village. Caroline Harding has been arrested."

"Shall I come with you?"

"You could, but it's probably not worth your while. She's being held at the police station there, and I need to question her."

"Have you found evidence that she poisoned her father?"

"There's no evidence to suggest that anyone else did, let's put it that way. And I'd also say that she had the means, motive and opportunity. Anyway, I need to go and see what she has to say for herself."

I felt disappointed that he didn't want me to accompany him, but there was little use in waiting around at the police station. "Could you ask someone to help me find Miss Brown's mother?" I asked.

"Not at the moment, I'm afraid. And besides, I'm not really sure it's a police matter."

"A young girl was taken away from her family, James! Her mother reported it to the police, but they did nothing about it."

"Millicent Brown's mother?"

"Yes!"

"That doesn't sound pleasant at all, but I'm rather tied up at the moment, Penny. Can this wait until after I've spoken to Caroline Harding? I also need to speak to the scientist who's been analysing the crockery and cutlery Mr Wigmore used on the evening of his death. Apparently, he has some interesting results for me."

A constable entered the room. "Are you ready, sir?" He gave me a sidelong glance, as if querying my presence.

"I am, Wilson. I'll see you this evening, Penny."

"Yes. I'll see you then, James." I left his office feeling I'd been coolly dismissed.

On returning home, I sat at my writing desk and felt sorry for myself for a while. My typewriter seemed redundant now that I no longer worked as a reporter. There were plenty of other publications I could write for, but that would mean contacting all the editors and informing them I was available for commissions. I struggled to find the motivation needed to carry out that sort of work. I felt weary.

The book I had been writing about my father's career in Amazonia was still incomplete, but I had lost interest in that too. His propensity for selfish behaviour had planted a seed of resentment within me.

I gazed out of the window, envying James his interesting job. I wondered if Scotland Yard would ever consider employing a lady detective. I reasoned that even if they did, it was unlikely that a married lady detective would ever be permitted.

A small mew of acknowledgement sounded behind me, and I turned to see Tiger strolling into the room. I extended my hand to her, and she rubbed her little head against it, eyes half closed. As I stroked the warm, soft fur on her back, I felt an unmistakable quickening sensation in my stomach.

I held my breath.

There it was again, like the tickle of a feather.

I clasped my hands to my stomach and felt tears welling in my eyes.

I had been harbouring suspicions for a while but had kept them to myself. They had finally been confirmed.

CHAPTER 36

I felt the need for some fresh air. I put on my hat and overcoat, then headed out into the chilly October afternoon. As I walked along the streets toward Parliament Hill, I encountered a number of infants and young children. Some were being pushed in perambulators, while others toddled on unsteady legs, grasping the hand of a mother or nursemaid. *Had there always been this many about, and I simply hadn't noticed them before?*

I had never desired to have children, and at the age of thirty-seven I'd assumed my childbearing years were most likely behind me. James had never expressed a particular wish for them either, knowing how important my work was to me. I had made that abundantly clear to him before we married.

What would he make of the news? It would be an enormous surprise for him. I smiled as I pictured disbelief on his face, followed by a wide grin. I felt sure he would be happy about becoming a father.

He would be a good father.

As I walked, I realised I possessed a secret that no one else could possibly know. An elderly lady smiled as she passed, and I realised she was returning the smile that lingered on my face. Although I was unsure yet what I thought about the prospect of motherhood, I instinctively felt a sense of joy.

The fatigue I'd been feeling in recent weeks made sense now. There had been a reason for it, and I felt relieved that it wasn't some sort of serious illness.

I decided to rest when I returned home, and Mrs Oliver had to wake me for dinner.

"Is James back?" I asked.

"No, something must have detained him. Would you like to eat now? I can keep his food warm for him. Or perhaps you'd like to dine together when he returns."

I told her I would wait until he returned and picked up a book to occupy the time. It was difficult to concentrate on the text. Instead, I kept concocting the evening's conversation in my mind. *Would it be best to wait until he had told me about his day? Or would it be better to tell him as soon as he returned? How would I phrase it?*

Seven o'clock came and went.

"I'll have to get going soon, Mrs Blakely," said Mrs Oliver, "or would you like me to wait until Mr Blakely gets home?"

"No, there's no need to wait. Thank you, Mrs Oliver. He gets held up with his work sometimes, as you know."

It was true that he could be quite late back on occasion, although he usually sent a telegram if he were likely to be delayed for a long while. Our plates remained on the sideboard, silver domes covering them to keep the food warm.

I began to feel restless once Mrs Oliver had left. *Why hadn't James sent a message?* It was almost eight o'clock. He had seemed quite irritable when I had called on him at the Yard, but that had been because he was busy and I had bothered him about something which could have waited.

I paced the room for a little while, then occupied my time feeding sardines to Tiger. She enjoyed them so much that she spent some time afterwards cleaning her face and paws. I watched her as I tried to ignore the pounding beat of my heart.

Nine o'clock came, and I wondered if there was anything I could do. Perhaps James had sent a telegram and it had been delivered to the wrong house. I reasoned that the unintended recipient would almost certainly have put it through the letterbox. *Perhaps no one had been at home when the messenger boy called and it was sitting on the doormat of an empty house.* I put on my overcoat, went out and called at my neighbours' houses. No one had received a telegram for me.

On my return, the house felt cold and dingy without James. I put some more coal on the fire and tried to reassure myself that he was fine. But I knew people could become quite unpredictable when backed into a corner.

Had James cornered someone? I could only think of Caroline Harding, and I couldn't see any way that she might do him harm. However, I knew from experience that investigations, and the suspects involved in them, had a propensity to be erratic.

The clock on the mantelpiece struck half-past nine, and I struggled to believe that James wasn't in some sort of trouble. My stomach felt knotted and my heart pounded. I knew I had to calm myself for the sake of the little life growing inside me. But it would be impossible to do so until I felt I was doing something about it.

Having decided to visit Scotland Yard for the second time that day, I hailed a cab on Finchley Road.

"Cold night to be out, madam," the cab driver commented as I climbed in. The streets were dark and quiet, so the horse made good progress, covering the distance in half an hour.

I disembarked, crossed the puddle-strewn yard and made my way toward the welcoming light of the reception area.

"I'll find out where he's got to, Mrs Blakely," responded the sergeant behind the desk when I enquired after James.

Silence descended as I watched him disappear through the door behind him.

A clop of boots sounded on the staircase shortly afterwards and a constable came into view. He doffed his helmet, bid me goodnight and stepped out through the door. *Was anyone else here worried about James?* Feeling lightheaded, I seated myself on a chair beside the door.

Eventually, the sergeant reappeared. "I believe he travelled to Dulwich this morning."

"Yes, he did," I snapped, irritated that he had no new information for me. "He was intending to question a woman there, Mrs Caroline Harding. He most likely met with Inspector Bridges of P Division." I recalled the red-cheeked man with the fleshy nose and barrel-shaped chest, whom I had met at Farley Lodge after Mr Wigmore's death. "Did my husband not return here after his trip to Dulwich?"

"I don't know, but I can try to find out for you." He disappeared behind the door again.

A short while later, another constable emerged from the office and went up the staircase. I wondered if he had been dispatched to find out more. It was ten minutes before he returned, and he briefly nodded at me before heading back inside the office.

Then the sergeant reappeared. "Perhaps you'd be more comfortable in the waiting room, Mrs Blakely."

I knew the Scotland Yard premises reasonably well, but I had never associated the place with comfort. The wood panelling and wooden seating served a practical purpose rather than a cosy one.

"Haven't you found him yet?" I asked.

"We're still trying to establish his whereabouts."

"He didn't return here after his Dulwich trip?"

"He doesn't appear to have done."

I felt a horrible weight shifting about in my stomach.

"Let me show you into the waiting room, Mrs Blakely. I'm sure there's a simple explanation as to his whereabouts. We just need to establish what it is."

"Can you get a message to Inspector Bridges of P Division and ask him?"

"Yes, we can do that."

I was half tempted to travel to Dulwich and make my own enquiries there.

Flames crackled in the waiting room fireplace. Wooden benches lined two of the walls, and chairs had been placed at a small, round table. I chose to sit at the table, where the chairs had some cushioning. Though worn, they looked more comfortable than the wooden seats.

"I'll bring you some tea," said the sergeant before departing.

I rested my head on the table and tried to slow my breathing. The recollection that James carried a revolver about with him was of some consolation to me. *But what if someone had taken it and used it against him?*

I took an even deeper breath and scolded myself for imagining the worst. There had to be a simple explanation for his disappearance. The sergeant didn't seem unduly worried. *Was he merely pretending, so as not to alarm me?*

CHAPTER 37

I drank the tea, watched the clock on the wall and tried to think of every possible explanation for James's disappearance. Eliza had once been on an underground train that had developed a fault and halted in a tunnel for four hours. I prayed James was running late for no reason other than a broken-down train. *But if that were the case, surely Scotland Yard would have figured it out by now.*

Brisk footsteps sounded in the corridor as the little hand on the clock approached eleven.

James?

I held my breath for a moment.

A few seconds later, a man in a dark suit entered the room. He had short brown hair, hooded eyes and a large, bushy moustache. I recognised him as the assistant commissioner, William Russell.

"Mrs Blakely," he said, "no need to get up. I'll join you at the table."

Mr Russell's presence suggested to me that James's disappearance was being taken more seriously now. My heart started racing again.

"Please don't worry yourself," he said, sensing the rising panic within me. "We'll sort this out. Your husband is an extremely capable inspector, and I'm sure no harm has come to him."

"Has there been any word from Inspector Bridges?" I asked.

"Yes, we've been in communication with Dulwich police station. They confirmed that he visited him there today and left at approximately four o'clock this afternoon."

"Four o'clock?" I glanced at the wall clock again. "That was seven hours ago!"

"It was indeed, and I would be lying, Mrs Blakely, if I were to say that I wasn't at all concerned. It's a little out of character for your husband."

"Very out of character! Have there been any problems with the trains from Dulwich today?"

"Not that I know of. Please rest assured that we have a number of chaps out looking for him and making enquiries. He's a popular and respected colleague here at the Yard, and we're all concerned for his well-being."

"Has there been any word from the hospitals?"

"They're being checked as we speak. As I'm sure you're aware, the role of an inspector can be quite unpredictable. It's not uncommon for one of my men to find himself waylaid somewhere from time to time. Sometimes the reason can seem quite obscure, but it's usually benign. All the London divisions have been notified and will be keeping an eye out for him. We have eyes everywhere, Mrs Blakely."

He smiled, which I guessed was supposed to be reassuring, but I couldn't feel reassured by anything while James remained missing.

"Now, I think the best thing for you, Mrs Blakely, would be to go home and wait there for news rather than sitting in this draughty old place. I've asked my dear wife to accompany you. Please rest assured that as soon as we have any news we'll have a messenger bring you a note or a telegram, whichever the quickest mode of communication might be."

"But I want to go and look for him," I protested.

"I understand that, Mrs Blakely, but it's late. I hope you don't mind me commenting in such a personal fashion, but you seem a little fatigued. I recommend that you try to rest for a while. I realise that's probably not the advice you were hoping to receive from me."

It wasn't, but for the sake of my own and my baby's health, I knew it was a sensible plan.

Mrs Russell arrived at the station a few minutes later. She looked to be about fifty years of age. Her grey hair was curled beneath a burgundy velvet hat and she wore a fur-trimmed overcoat.

"Hello, Mrs Blakely." She had the manner of a nurse, and I wondered if she had ever worked in that profession. "Let's get you home, where you'll be warmer and more comfortable. I can sit with you until your husband returns."

"Thank you, Mrs Russell, although I'm sure there's no need for you to sit with me. I shall be all right."

"Does anyone else live there with you?"

"We have a housekeeper, but she doesn't live in."

"In that case, I think it's best if I stay with you."

I was unaccustomed to accepting any help, but on this occasion I acquiesced. Tired and extremely concerned about James, it would have been foolish to turn down her kind offer. And, in the unthinkable event that I received bad news, at least I would have someone with me.

I got up from my seat and steadied myself against the table.

Mrs Russell took my arm. "It won't take us long to get to

St John's Wood," she said. "The roads are quiet at this time of night."

I closed my eyes for a moment. I felt as if I were on a never-ending carousel, spinning around and around. I wanted it to stop.

I wanted everything to feel normal again.

CHAPTER 38

Daylight glimmered beyond the curtains when I awoke. I immediately hauled myself upright and looked at the clock. It had passed seven. Having lain awake for most of the night with Tiger beside me, I couldn't recall falling asleep. A hollow remained in the eiderdown where she had rested. I suspected she was downstairs, looking for her breakfast.

There was still no James.

His pillow lay next to mine, smooth and unruffled. I felt convinced that something awful had happened to him. Mrs Russell had probably received word while I slept and had been waiting downstairs to break the news to me when I woke up.

I staggered out of bed. My head felt heavy and a sour taste lingered in my mouth. I pushed the curtains aside and looked out at the grey, drizzly morning. The rooftops of the houses opposite glistened with rain, and a pigeon bathed itself in a large puddle that had formed in the road. I watched it for a moment, envious of its blissful ignorance.

I quickly washed at the washstand, dressed and made my way downstairs, holding on to the handrail as I went.

I heard voices from the dining room. Mrs Oliver had probably just arrived and Mrs Russell was no doubt telling her the sad news about James. After pausing in the hallway, I closed my eyes and prepared myself for what I was about to discover.

I felt a strange floating sensation as I walked into the dining room, as if my feet were somehow disconnected from my body. I pushed open the door to the dining room and there, drinking tea with Mrs Russell at the breakfast table, sat James.

I gasped.

He jumped to his feet. "Penny!"

I could immediately tell that he hadn't slept. Dark shadows circled his eyes and a layer of rough stubble covered his chin.

I rushed at him, flinging my arms around his neck. "Where've you been?"

He held me in his embrace for a moment, not saying a word. Then he patted my back and took a step back.

"Oh, it was just a complicated case I've been working on for some time." He looked away and rubbed at his brow.

"But what happened? Were you in danger? Who were you with?"

"A few unpleasant gentlemen I've been after for a while. Let's just say that they 'hosted' me for a few hours."

"Where?"

"In the East End." He gave my hand a squeeze. "If you don't mind, Penny, that's all I have to say on the matter for now, as the case is still ongoing. I haven't yet apprehended the person I was after, and I'm concerned that if I say too much at this stage, the case may be compromised."

"They held you against your will?" I queried. "You should

send some men down there right away and have them arrested!"

"It isn't as simple as that. I do have a plan, though, and it will all be resolved soon. In the meantime, I think you need some breakfast, Penny. You look tired, too, and I can't imagine you enjoyed much sleep. I'm so sorry about that."

"It doesn't sound as if any of it was your fault," I said, taking a seat at the table. I found that I felt ravenously hungry all of a sudden.

As I took a slice of toast from the toast rack, I wondered why James had told me so little about his ordeal. Perhaps Mrs Russell's presence was preventing him from doing so.

She rose to take her leave of us a short while later, and I thanked her profusely for all her help.

"That's quite all right, Mrs Blakely. I'm just relieved that Detective Inspector Blakely is returned safe and well."

"So am I!"

James went upstairs to wash and change, and then we sat down together in the front room. I expected him to tell me everything that had happened, but it wasn't to be.

"Sometimes there are elements of my work that must remain confidential," he said. "I'm sorry, Penny, but that's just how it has to be. Once this case is cracked, I'll be able to tell you everything. But for the time being, it must stay under wraps. I should have taken someone with me yesterday. That's all I've really learned from the experience."

"Did they threaten you? Did they actually harm you?"

"No. They just wanted to have an exceptionally long discussion that would keep me awake all night."

"And that's really all you can tell me?"

He leaned in closer and took my hand. "I wish I could tell you everything, Penny, I really do. But at the moment, it's quite impossible. You must trust me on that."

"All right, I do trust you. Just as long as you promise to tell me what happened as soon as you can."

"I will. In the meantime, there's no need for either of us to do any more work on the Jane Bunton case."

"Why's that?"

"It's become too complicated. We both need to leave it well alone."

"Does that have anything to do with what happened last night?"

He paused as he considered this. "In complete confidence, yes it does. I had quite an unpleasant encounter; one I hope never to experience again. And I certainly wouldn't want you to experience anything of the kind, Penny."

"But I'm very unlikely to, James. I'm hardly a detective inspector of Scotland Yard, am I?"

"No, but you have been making enquiries about the case, and that's more than enough for these people. We both need to stop poking around."

"But I can't just stop my work on the case. I've never been able to do that. I've seen every case I've worked on through to the very end."

"Well, you can't this time!"

I wanted a proper explanation, but I could see that I was not about to receive one. I knew James well enough to under-stand that pushing him would merely irritate him further. Perhaps it was time to share my news.

"James, I have something to tell you."

His eyebrows raised in interest. "What is it?"

"I'm with child." My eyes filled with tears as soon as I uttered the words.

He stared at me, then his jaw dropped open before quickly closing again. A broad grin spread across his face. "Really?"

I nodded.

"But I thought you had no wish to become a mother?"

"So did I!" I laughed, a tear rolling down my cheek. "But now I think I might like to after all."

He stood and stepped over to my chair. "Oh, Penny, this is wonderful news. So wonderful."

For the first time since I had known him, I saw that there were tears in his eyes. I got up from my seat and we embraced again.

"Are you happy about it?" I ventured.

"Happy? I'm overjoyed!"

CHAPTER 39

After a brief rest, James readied himself to return to Scotland Yard. "There's still a jewel thief to catch," he said. "I've been so distracted by the recent murders that the Hatton Garden case has been rather neglected for the past week or so."

"Must you go back to work today?"

"Yes, I really must. I'll get some more rest this evening."

"But what about the men who detained you last night?"

"Oh, we don't need to worry about them any longer."

"What makes you so sure?"

"Because I'll be focusing on the jewel thief case from now on."

"They specifically told you to stop working on the Jane Bunton case?"

His silence confirmed my suspicion.

"But that's ridiculous!" I exclaimed. "They can't be allowed to stop the mechanics of justice by going around threatening people!"

"I really can't discuss it any further at the moment."

"Well, I'm going to continue with my work on the case."

"No, Penny, you mustn't." His voice was low, yet commanding.

"Why not?"

"Because you simply cannot afford to put yourself at risk. You've done so in the past, and I have reluctantly stood by and allowed it. But it's impossible for me to do that now. Things have changed."

"But I don't want to stop, James. I need to find out who murdered Mrs Bunton."

"We all want to find that out, Penny, but there's a lot of unpleasant business taking place right now. You and I need to stay well away from it. It would be irresponsible of me as a husband and father to allow you to continue with the work you've been doing."

"*Allow* me? We established at the outset of our marriage that you would never try to control my work."

"But you're expecting a baby! It's much too dangerous."

"Until you tell me exactly what happened last night, James, I shall refuse to comply. It isn't fair to tell me I can no longer work on the case without giving me a proper explanation. I can't understand why you're refusing to tell me. I'm your wife! Why the secrecy all of a sudden? We need to seek justice for the victims and their families, but I'm worried you're willing to let it go now that you've been threatened, and then the murderers will get away with it."

"I'm doing this in our best interests, and in the interests of our unborn child. Please take my word for it, Penny. You can't just think about yourself any more."

I felt offended by the suggestion that I was being selfish. "But I'm not only thinking about myself! And besides, if you've been threatened, that's a crime in itself. You need to have these people arrested, James. They shouldn't be allowed to get away with it."

"My colleagues are dealing with all that. It's best that you and I forget about it for now."

"What if Jane Bunton's murderer is never apprehended?"

"We can't solve every single case in the manner we'd like, Penny. We've been fortunate enough to find the person responsible in all the previous cases you and I have worked on together. But there are a good many cases that are never resolved. It's difficult, but sometimes we must accept it."

"Well, there's nothing to stop me looking for Millicent Brown's family," I replied.

James rolled his eyes. "I still don't think it's safe."

"Miss Brown clearly needs help."

"Perhaps, but not necessarily yours. You cannot try to solve every problem or to seek justice for every wrong, Penny. You really should stay away from all this. Why not start packing your things, ready for your trip to Liverpool tomorrow? The good news is, I can accompany you now that I'm no longer working on the Jane Bunton case."

I felt tired, yet restless, after James left. It didn't seem right to be doing nothing to help solve the murder case, and it angered me that James had given in to threats so easily. *Surely Scotland Yard wouldn't stand for one of their officers being threatened.*

I wondered what was happening about Caroline Harding. *Was she still being held by the police? And what of Samuel Bunton and his alleged affair with Mrs Hargreaves? And how did Edith Jones, who had borrowed all that money and not paid it back, fit in to all this?*

My jaw clenched with frustration. There were so many lines of enquiry, but no one to follow them up. And to exacerbate matters, we were due to leave for Liverpool in the morning. *Could I achieve anything worthwhile in such a short space of time?*

I recalled Samuel Bunton mentioning that he had found some men of his own to work on the case. *Were these the same men who had threatened James?*

I had a lot of unanswered questions, and there were several people I wanted to speak to, but I knew it would be foolhardy to completely ignore James's advice. He had clearly been through an unpleasant experience; so unpleasant, in fact, that he had deemed it necessary to protect me from the details.

There had to be some sort of quiet research I could do. I decided that my search for Millicent Brown's family could continue in one of my favourite places: the reading room at the British Library.

"Penny!" Francis whispered, greeting me with a broad smile. "Anything I can help you with today?"

"I need to find a family in Camden," I whispered in reply, "and I should like to consult some of the directories you have here."

"Of course."

I knew where the directories were kept, but Francis escorted me over to them anyway.

"Are you planning another excursion to Dulwich anytime soon?" he asked. "I enjoyed our little jaunt there last week."

"I'm not, I'm afraid."

"That's a shame. Anywhere else of interest?"

"No." I could hear the despondent tone in my voice. "Just Liverpool, I suppose. Are you looking forward to that?"

"Oh yes, Liverpool." He scratched his temple. "Now, which directory did you say it was? Camden?"

"That's right."

He pulled the relevant directory from the shelf. "And the name?"

"Brown."

"Brown? Oh dear!" He flicked through the directory. "Have you any idea how many Browns there are here? It must be the second-most popular surname after Smith."

"Surely Jones is."

"That's a good point; it could be Jones. Nonetheless, we have hundreds of Browns here. Any idea whereabouts in Camden?"

"Near the railway station might be a good place to start."

"In that case, you'll need a map, too." He handed me the directory and led me over to where the maps were displayed.

"Have you seen Eliza recently?" I asked. "She was in a bit of trouble with her employer when I saw her last."

"Oh, yes. I think that's resolved now." He thumbed through the maps on the shelf. "Here's Camden." He pulled it out and handed it to me. "Do you have everything you need now?"

"I do. Thank you, Francis."

"It's a pleasure, Penny." He grinned. "Always a pleasure."

I compiled a list of names and addresses using the directory and the map. Within an hour, I had found three families by the name of Brown who lived near the railway station, and a further twelve who lived within a mile's radius of it.

The problem was knowing what to do with the information. If I were to heed James's warning, I would need to stay away from the investigation altogether, but I couldn't help thinking about Millicent Brown's family and how they were being denied an opportunity to be reunited with their daughter and sister. Perhaps they were aware that she was being touted as a medium, but too scared to make an approach. If that were the case, I wondered what Professor Mortimer might have done to make them so fearful. The only chance I had of finding out was to speak to them myself.

I bid Francis farewell and left the reading room. As I

descended the steps of the British Museum, a thought came to my mind. Professor Mortimer had told me that the Brown family had spoken to the police about their daughter. The police station in Camden should have a record of this. If I could look at that, I would most likely be able to obtain the family's contact details. It would mean persuading James or another officer at the station to let me have a look, however, and that wouldn't be easy.

I passed through the gates and turned left onto Great Russell Street. *Might it be better to speak to the people on the list I had made rather than troubling the police for their records?* I couldn't imagine James being happy with either course of action.

I had no time to react to what happened next.

I was lifted from my feet by a strong assailant who had approached me from behind. In an instant, they bundled me into a carriage and forced me to the floor. I tried to lash out, but my arms were clasped behind my back and a rag placed over my nose and mouth. I kicked my feet, but firm hands held them still. At least two people restrained me.

The carriage jolted as it moved on. I tried my best to turn my head away from the rag, but to no avail. It carried the faint, sweet smell of cut grass.

Chloroform.

The more I struggled, the firmer I was held. I had been rendered powerless. I could do nothing other than succumb.

CHAPTER 40

I came round to find myself tethered to a chair in a small, dark room. My mouth felt dry and a dull pain throbbed in my head. I tried to move, but quickly ascertained that my wrists were bound behind me and my ankles had been tethered to the legs of the chair with strips of cloth. A thin rope had been wrapped around my abdomen, securing me firmly to the back of the chair. I worried about the little life growing within me. *Would he or she endure this? Who had done this to me? And how long had I been here?*

The room appeared to have no windows. Dimly lit by a flickering gas lamp, which was reflected in a mirror, it smelled of damp. As my eyes adjusted to the gloom, I noticed a rack of clothing beside the door and a dressing table in front of the mirror. One corner of the room had a curtain pulled across it. *Was I in a dressing room?*

My hat was resting on the table, presumably having come off in the struggle. My carpet bag lay on the floor a few feet away. Whoever had tied me to the chair was presumably waiting for me to wake up.

"Hello?" I called out.

There was no response.

I could only deduce that I was in the basement of a theatre. I wriggled my hands and body, hoping the tethers would come loose, but I had been tied up well. After some considerable time spent squirming and fidgeting, I reached the conclusion that I would not be able to free myself.

My movement had caused the chair to shift, however, and I realised that by lurching back and forth a little I could move forward an inch or two. I continued to do this for a while; remaining cautious, as I didn't want the chair to topple over. Before long, I noticed I could move my weight forward onto my feet, lift the rear legs of the chair and shuffle forward at a slightly quicker rate. It was arduous work – the tethers cut into my ankles, and I had to be careful not to fall – but, inch by inch, I managed to shuffle my way over to the door.

Once I had reached it, I sat back in the chair and rested for a moment. It was difficult to know what I had accomplished, but I felt I was at least doing something to resolve my situation rather than sitting back and doing nothing at all. I listened carefully for any sound that might give me a clue as to where I was or who might be nearby.

I heard nothing.

Would James have realised I was missing yet? I had no way of telling the time or how long I had been here. *Had anyone witnessed my kidnap?* It felt difficult to believe that I could be snatched away from a busy street without anyone noticing and raising the alarm.

The door had a lock, but was it actually locked? There was no way of opening it without first freeing my hands. I twisted and pulled until the cloth rubbed my wrists sore. I paused for a moment to catch my breath and calm myself. I considered my efforts so far and realised I'd been using all my strength to struggle with the ties around my wrists. Perhaps I could do better with less force.

I tried again, moving my hands more slowly in the hope that I could ease the binds down over them. I rubbed one wrist against the other in a careful movement and was eventually rewarded as I felt the ties move a little lower. I persevered for some time, my shoulders and arms aching all the while. It became more difficult when the tethers reached the widest part of my hand, at the base of my thumb. Panic rose as I feared I would never be free. I calmed myself once again and tried to envisage narrowing and elongating my hands to allow the ties to slip over them.

Just as I had convinced myself that I would remain stuck in that position forever, another tug freed my right hand. I laughed to myself, relieved that my hard work had paid off. The tie on my left hand immediately loosened, and suddenly both hands were free.

At that moment, I felt gripped with a fear that someone would walk into the room and scupper my plan to break free. I had to find the end of the rope wrapped around my middle. I felt about frantically and found that it was knotted at the back of the chair. My arms and shoulders ached as I tried to twist them into a position that would allow me to untie it, having no choice but to rest at regular intervals. All the while, I had a growing anxiety that my escape attempt would soon be discovered. I had little doubt that the people who had imprisoned me would be angry when they saw what I had achieved.

I felt a renewed sense of urgency as I picked at the rope knot. Now that I had begun my escape, I needed to complete it before my captors turned up. My fingertips felt sore as they picked at the rope. It briefly reminded me of the time I had spent picking oakum at Shoreditch Workhouse while I was working on a double murder case. After a while, the knot in the rope budged and I could untie it.

I bent forward and set to work on my tethered ankles.

They were bound with strips of cotton, perhaps torn from a bedsheet or shirt. The knots had been tightened by my movements across the floor. In hindsight, I wondered why I had done that before attempting to free myself.

My petticoats and skirt got in the way as I tried to see what I was doing. The knots finally loosened under my sore fingertips, and I could barely suppress my glee as I leapt up out of the chair, free at last.

I pushed the chair into the corner and tried the door handle. The door was locked, as I had suspected. I stepped over to the curtain and pulled it to one side, hoping it concealed another door or window. There was nothing behind it but a small area for changing.

I scoured the floor, looking for a trapdoor, but there was no means of escape. I looked up at the ceiling in the hope that there might be a hatch, but it wasn't to be.

I paced up and down. *How would I ever get out of this room?* I figured I could lie in wait at the door and bring the chair down onto my captor's head when he or she entered the room. I walked over to the door and picked up the chair, readying myself. Although I considered this a reasonable plan, its success was reliant on my captor turning up relatively soon. If the kidnapper did not appear for many hours, it would be a long wait, poised with the chair.

I realised a hatpin could double as another possible weapon. One had remained in my hair, despite my hat coming off. I put the chair down for a moment, pulled out the hatpin and tucked it inside the pocket of my skirt.

Standing by the door with the chair in my hands once again, I glanced about the room and wondered if there was some other trap I could set. Perhaps I could tie the rope to the door handle, triggering something to fall on my captors as they opened the door. To do that, I would need something heavy, and I would have to suspend it above the door somehow. I couldn't see how that might be achieved.

I soon grew tired of standing poised with the chair. I decided to search the room once more for anything that might be useful. I propped the chair up against the door and wedged its back beneath the handle. I hoped this would make any attempted entry to the room difficult, giving me time to prepare while my captor unlocked and attempted to open the door.

With the chair propped up against the door, I felt a little more in control of my situation. I searched the room more closely and examined the clothing on the rack. There were several old jackets and pairs of trousers, and a few elaborate dresses, one of which was torn at the shoulder. Pots of pearl powder and Macassar oil sat on the dressing table next to an old ivory-handled hairbrush. I rested my hand on the table, feeling dust between my fingertips when I lifted it again.

The mirror above the dressing table was spotted with damp, and my face stared back at me, ghostly pale in the gloom. There were three drawers in the dressing table. I opened each in turn to find another hairbrush, a number of hairnets, some rouge and a pot of cold cream.

The third drawer contained a diary from 1882. I flicked through it, reading the entries about auditions and rehearsals inked in spidery writing. It felt tempting to spend a good while looking through it in greater detail, but my eye suddenly glimpsed something bronze in the drawer.

A key.

I seized it and dashed over to the door. I pulled the chair away, then pushed the key into the lock. It fitted!

A combination of excitement and trepidation surged through me as I turned the key in the lock.

I had freed myself, but who – or what – was waiting on the other side of the door?

I slowly turned the handle, pulled the door open an inch and cautiously peered out. My view was of a low-ceilinged, whitewashed corridor. I felt sure I had seen the place before.

Was I inside the Theatre Royal Drury Lane?

I stepped out into the corridor, feeling vulnerable and exposed. I needed to get out of here as quickly as possible.

To my right was a staircase, so I headed in that direction.

A voice from behind stopped me in my tracks.

"I underestimated you, Mrs Blakely!"

CHAPTER 41

I turned to see Professor Mortimer standing there.

"I was just on my way to pay you a visit," he said. "It seems I was almost too late."

He took a step toward me and I edged back in the direction of the staircase. I didn't want him to come too close.

"There are some wonderful tunnels running beneath this theatre," he continued, "constructed more than two hundred years ago. One of them leads down to the river, and in the past it enabled King Charles II to meet his mistress, the actress Nell Gwynne. He would arrive by boat, enter the tunnel at the river, and then make his way up to the royal box in this theatre. As soon as the lights were dimmed for the performance, he would make his way over to another tunnel; one that leads to the public house across the road, where his mistress would be conveniently located."

I was in no mood for a history lesson. "Why did you bring me here?" I demanded.

"I wanted to have a discussion with you."

"What about?"

"About your strange obsession with me and Miss Shelley."

"I merely wish to pursue justice, Professor."

"You have a peculiar way of going about it."

"More peculiar than kidnapping a young girl, putting her on the stage and pretending she can communicate with the spirit world?"

He laughed. "It's called *entertainment*, Mrs Blakely."

"It's not quite so entertaining for Elizabeth Shelley, though, is it? Or perhaps I should use her proper name, Millicent Brown."

"She has benefited enormously from her fame and is now in a position to help her family."

"But you've made her an accessory to murder. That's why you brought me here, isn't it? You murdered Jane Bunton. And to make matters worse, you dragged that poor innocent girl into it."

"She ran away before I fired the revolver, just as I had instructed her to."

"That doesn't change the fact that you subjected her to a dreadful ordeal. How will she ever recover, knowing that she was involved in Mrs Bunton's death?"

"She's a resilient young woman. And besides, she understood the necessity of it."

"There is never a need to commit murder!"

"Jane Bunton was threatening our livelihood."

"Nonsense! I saw how many people attended your show. Admirable though Jane's protest was, she wasn't doing any real harm."

"But her protests were beginning to have an effect. Our ticket sales were declining. That Bunton woman had a lot to answer for!"

"Sales were declining because the public had begun to realise that your act is an outrageous fraud. Ridding the world of Jane Bunton was never going to change that, and murdering her was a senseless act. How did you ever think you'd get away with it?"

He shrugged. "It was a dark, foggy night, and I hoped no one would see us. Other than Mrs Bunton, of course. I don't think you understand how much of a nuisance she was making of herself. Not only was she handing around leaflets outside our shows, but she had also sent countless letters accusing me of fraud and deception. Whenever we put on a show, she was there. Elizabeth found it deeply upsetting. She just wouldn't leave us alone. We were so tired of her. And I must say that I'm growing quite tired of you as well, Mrs Blakely. Your husband was much more compliant."

"You were the one behind James's disappearance?"

He laughed. "He didn't *disappear*; we were just having a nice long discussion. He cares very deeply about you, doesn't he? I only had to mention your name, and he immediately agreed to all my demands."

"Why snatch me off the street, then?"

"You refused to heed his warning. I wanted to ensure that you'd be frightened enough to stay at home, but when one of my men saw you going about your business as if nothing had happened, I decided we had to do something about you."

Too fearful to ask what he planned to do with me, I changed the subject. "When Miss Brown announced to the theatre that the murderer was present, she meant you, didn't she? That was her confession."

"Nonsense!"

"What was the plan? Because it didn't go to plan, did it?"

He shifted his weight uncomfortably.

"What name did you tell her to announce? Mr Bunton? Mrs Harding, perhaps? Miss Jones? She couldn't bring herself to lie, but she wasn't brave enough to name you, either, and now I understand why. Instead, she told us all that the culprit was in the room. I should have realised she was talking about you at the time."

He sniffed the air, then smiled. "I smell lavender. Do you smell lavender, Mrs Blakely?"

"No." I did feel a sudden chill, however.

"Perhaps it's the Lavender Lady. Have you heard of her? She's one of the spirits who haunts this place. It's said that whenever she's around, a strong scent of lavender appears in the air and the temperature drops. You sense it, don't you, Mrs Blakely? Don't try to deny it."

"You're not frightening me, you know."

He started walking toward me, and I quickly turned to climb the stairs.

"Come back, Mrs Blakely! We haven't finished our conversation."

"We can continue it elsewhere."

When I reached the top of the steps, I found myself in the wings. I was about to walk onto the stage when a figure stepped in front of me.

Richard Fairchild, the theatre manager.

"I think Professor Mortimer wanted to continue his conversation with you," he stated. The twitch I had noticed before lifted the left side of his face, giving him a sinister expression.

Had he been listening in the entire time?

I moved to step past him, but he blocked my way. "I would cooperate if I were you, Mrs Blakely. Otherwise, you might end up tied to that chair again."

I turned back and saw that Professor Mortimer had reached the top of the staircase. They had me cornered.

"Surely you feel the spirits now, don't you, Mrs Blakely?" asked the professor, his features barely discernible in the gloom. "It's on this very stage that the ghost of Joey Grimaldi guides and steers the actors about."

"Let me go!" I demanded. "My husband will already be out looking for me."

"But he has no idea where you are. That's a shame, isn't it?"

"What do you want from me?"

"To be completely frank with you, Mrs Blakely, there is nothing I want from you. You've become a considerable nuisance to me, just as Jane Bunton did."

Nausea swum in my stomach. I couldn't afford to show either man that I was scared. "You can't hurt me," I said, "or my unborn child."

The professor blinked for a moment, clearly surprised to hear these words.

The man was clearly barbaric, but was it possible that he might spare me for the sake of my baby?

It seemed not.

He seized my right arm and began pulling me back toward the staircase. I struggled, trying to pull away, but he was too strong. I was forced to stagger down the stairs with him, worried that if I resisted I would slip and fall. I could hear the manager's footsteps echoing behind me.

I assumed the professor intended to take me back to the dressing room and lock me in there again, and I couldn't bear the thought of it. *What was James doing now? How would anyone find me here?*

Professor Mortimer's grip on my arm was strong, but I knew I had to do something. *Was there any chance that I could escape these two men, or would it be foolhardy to try?* From the sound of it, the professor wasn't about to let me go again. I had to save myself, whatever it took.

I reached into my pocket with my left hand and retrieved the hatpin. In one swift movement, I jabbed it into the professor's arm.

He screeched as the pin pierced his jacket sleeve and dug its way into his flesh. He recoiled and loosened his grip. I skipped away from him.

"You witch!" he hissed, pulling the hatpin from his arm. Then he lunged forward and managed to grab me again. He pulled my hair, and I yelped with pain.

"Get hold of her, Fairchild!" he shouted at the manager.

I knew I stood no chance against the pair of them. I tried to release my hair from his hand, but he pulled harder. I felt relieved to notice that the manager hadn't stepped forward to help.

"Fairchild!" the professor shouted again. "We need to stop this nonsense and get her back to the dressing room!"

He held the hatpin inches from my face, pointing it threateningly near one of my eyes. "Let's stop struggling, Mrs Blakely. You don't want to spoil your pretty features, do you?"

"Let me go!" I protested. "For the sake of my baby!"

From the corner of my eye, I saw Richard Fairchild step forward. I knew that I was done for. Professor Mortimer had felt no qualms about murdering Jane Bunton, and he no doubt cared just as little for my life and the life of my child. I stopped struggling and resigned myself to my fate, waiting to see what the pair would do to me now.

Professor Mortimer gasped as Richard Fairchild flung an arm around his neck and held him tight in a lock.

"This has gone on long enough, Mortimer!" he hissed. "You can't do this to a lady. Especially not a lady in such a delicate condition!" Then he looked at me. "Run, Mrs Blakely!" he ordered. "Get out of here, as fast as you can!"

I turned and did as he had said. Through a maze of corridors I stumbled, sobbing as I went. *Was I really about to escape?* Despite my blurred vision, I managed to find a steep iron staircase leading down to a door. I dashed down the steps, pushed the door open and fell out into the street.

CHAPTER 42

"I made him swear not to go near you, Penny!" fumed James, pacing the floor of our bedroom. "And he gave me his word! Then he went and—"

"James!" Eliza interrupted. "Anger isn't going to change anything. You need to calm down for Penelope's sake." She sat down at my bedside, holding my hand. "Besides, your colleagues have arrested him now. He'll never know freedom again."

"And I'm fine," I piped up. "Just a bit tired. I don't even need to be in bed any more."

"Yes, you do," asserted Eliza. "Your well-being is very important now that you're nurturing a new life, Penelope."

"Are you saying that it wasn't important before?"

"It's even more important now. I don't think you'll be well enough to travel to Liverpool tomorrow."

"But I want to go! I don't know if, or when, I'll see Father again."

"You need to stay in bed for a while," she replied.

I hauled myself up into a sitting position. "I'm not lying in bed until next spring!"

"No, that would never do," added James.

"You're supposed to be looking after your wife in her vulnerable condition," scolded Eliza.

"Oh, but I'll never get a moment's peace if I insist that Penny spends the next few months in bed!"

"That's right," I agreed. "I would make life thoroughly miserable for you if you insisted on it."

Eliza rolled her eyes.

"What's happened to Miss Brown?" I asked James.

"She's been arrested."

"No!"

"Oh, Penelope, you mustn't get yourself agitated," my sister warned. "It's bad for your health."

"But Miss Brown was forced to comply with Professor Mortimer's plan!" I protested. "She should be treated as a victim, not a criminal."

"I agree," said James, "and for that reason I shall visit my colleagues in Camden this evening to inform them. I shall also ask them to track down Miss Brown's family so we can determine whether she can return to them."

"Thank you, James. Do you remember the performance we attended when she supposedly claimed to have contacted the spirit of Jane Bunton? She said that the murderer was in the theatre. She was referring to Professor Mortimer! It was her way of telling us."

"If only she'd been braver a little sooner."

"He obviously threatened her. How else could he have persuaded her to be involved in the murder and then lie for him afterwards? She must be treated with compassion by the police."

"We'll give her the opportunity to fully explain herself. If she was frightened of Professor Mortimer, she certainly has nothing to fear from him any more."

"We shouldn't be discussing all this now," said Eliza. "Penelope needs to rest."

"As for the theatre manager, Mr Fairchild," James said, ignoring her completely. "I was surprised to discover that he was such a close friend of the professor."

"If it hadn't been for his intervention, who knows what Professor Mortimer would have done to me?" I shuddered, feeling certain that the professor had been close to committing murder a second time.

"I'm just pleased you're safe now, Penny." James leaned forward and gave me a kiss. "There's interesting news from Dulwich, too," he added. "It appears that Mr Wigmore may not have been murdered after all, but instead carried out an act of self-destruction."

"How awful!" exclaimed my sister. "But as I said before, we shouldn't be discussing such subjects while Penelope is trying to recuperate."

"How extremely sad," I said. "Is there any proof?"

"A letter he left in his room," replied James. "It seems it had slipped off a table and was found beneath a chair. It's been closely examined, and the experts have confirmed that it was written in his own hand. He had grown tired of his frailty and poor health, and his daughter's death had proved too much for him to bear."

"Poor Mr Wigmore. I never met him, but the whole situation saddens me enormously. I can't imagine the depth of despair he must have felt." I wiped a tear from my eye. "And what of Samuel Bunton? I expect he was happy to hear that Professor Mortimer has been arrested again."

"I expect he was. We were wrong to suspect him."

"He didn't help himself by marching over here and shouting at you. He should have left you to get on with your work."

"I suppose he was frustrated."

"Why didn't your colleagues arrest Professor Mortimer after your overnight encounter with him?" I asked.

"I told them not to. He'd threatened to harm you, Penny, and he'd already murdered one young woman."

"But if they'd arrested him, he wouldn't have been able to!"

"You saw the men he had working for him. We met a few of them in the corridor at the theatre that time, didn't we? He would have given them the order before we had a chance to arrest them all. I believe the Yard has apprehended the whole gang now, but we'll need to make sure so we know that you're completely safe."

"How terrifying!" commented Eliza. "I'm just so relieved that you're about to become a mother, Penelope. You'll have to stop all this nonsense you keep getting yourself caught up in."

"I shall still write my articles, Ellie."

"Even though you no longer work for the *Morning Express?*"

"Absolutely. Perhaps I shall choose safer subjects from now on, but nothing will ever stop me writing. You can count on that."

CHAPTER 43

We met Eliza and Mrs Garnett beside the statue of George Stephenson in the Great Hall of Euston Station the following morning. James insisted on carrying my trunk for me, and I decided not to argue about it. Although I felt perfectly capable of doing everything for myself, I understood his desire to look after me.

"Thank goodness you're here!" my sister said.

"We still have half an hour before our train leaves, Ellie."

"Yes, I know that, but I still worry about these things. There could always be a last-minute hiccup."

"Sometimes they change the time of the train," said Mrs Garnett. "I've had that before."

"Oh, don't say that," Eliza groaned. "Now I'll need to go and check it again."

"If they're going to change it, it'll be later, not earlier," I said. "Otherwise it wouldn't be fair on people, would it?"

"Sometimes they've no intention of being fair on people," said Mrs Garnett. "That's the railway companies for you. Just as long as we don't crash, I'll be happy. Did you hear about that accident in Yorkshire earlier this year? An axle from the wagon of a coal train broke and the train came off its rails, crashing into another one! Four people killed and scores injured."

"Oh, don't!" wailed Eliza.

"I shall enjoy our journey up to Liverpool far more with that thought in my mind," said James wryly.

"Where's Francis?" I asked, realising we were still waiting for him.

Eliza looked down at her hands. "He's not coming."

"Not coming? But I only saw him yesterday, and he said nothing to that eff—"

"He paid me a visit yesterday evening," she added, "after I'd come to see you." Her voice cracked.

"But what reason did he give? He and Father always got on well, didn't they? I assumed he would want to see him again."

"He's thinking of visiting him in Amazonia instead."

"What?" I stared at Eliza, wondering whether I could truly believe what she was saying. "How? And when?"

"Why don't you ask him yourself?" said James, looking over my shoulder.

I turned to see Francis striding towards us. He had no luggage with him.

"Good morning," he said. "I thought I'd come and see you all off."

"Thank you, Francis," replied Eliza sombrely.

"You're not coming to Liverpool with us?" I asked.

"No." He scratched the back of his neck awkwardly. "I paid a visit to your dear sister last night and explained myself. I intend to take another journey instead."

"Where are you heading?"

"I'm not sure yet, but I've bought a ticket to Paris. From

there I'll travel through France and Italy before boarding a boat to Africa."

"Africa?"

"Probably Egypt, to begin with. Then I may travel south through Africa or head east. I haven't made up my mind just yet."

"But what about your job?"

"Today is my last day at the library." He checked his watch. "In fact, I'd better get going in just a moment. It wouldn't do to be late."

"But you *love* that job," I replied, unable to hide my surprise.

"I do enjoy it," he said, pushing his spectacles up his nose, "but I don't want to spend the rest of my life stuck in a library. Perhaps they'll take me back in a few years, once I've satisfied my urge to see the world."

"No doubt you'll have married a foreign lady by then," said Eliza bitterly.

Francis ran a hand through his hair, unsure how to reply.

Mrs Garnett wished him a safe journey.

"Thank you Mrs Garnett. And Eliza..." They held each other's gaze. "I feel that I've already said everything I wished to say yesterday evening..."

"And me, too." She stepped forward and gave him a warm embrace. "You will always be a dear friend, Francis."

"I shall return before you know it. Just you wait and see."

Eliza stepped back and pulled out her handkerchief. I felt a deep sorrow that she and Francis no longer planned to wed. There was little doubt that she would need our comfort on the train journey.

I turned to Francis. "You must write," I said. "Every week!" My voice choked and I could say no more. I embraced him.

"Goodbye, Penny. You're going to be a wonderful mother."

I pulled back from him. "How did you know about that?"

He smiled. "News travels fast."

"Goodbye, old chap," said James, stepping forward and shaking his hand. "I shan't embrace you, but I echo everything Penny said. You must write to us every week! We want to hear everything you're getting up to."

"If Mr Green decides to stay in Amazonia, I shall visit him there. It should be an exciting few years." He grinned.

I sensed he was happy with his decision, even if poor Eliza wasn't. "Be careful, Francis," I said. "We shall miss you."

"And I shall miss you, too," he replied. "More than you realise."

He doffed his hat, and I felt a lump in my throat as he walked away.

A whistle sounded from the platforms.

"That had better not be our train about to depart!" Mrs Garnett cried out.

"It won't be," said James, "but let's go and see all the same."

He picked up our luggage, and we headed for the archway that led through to the platforms.

"Are you looking forward to seeing your father again?" James asked me.

"Yes," I replied, feeling a little flutter in my stomach, as if the baby agreed with me. "No matter what he's done in the past, family will always be important to me. And it will be even more important when we have a family of our own."

James grinned, and we stepped into a haze of smoke and steam.

We were about to begin a big adventure of our own.

THE END

HISTORICAL NOTE

Communication with spirits was something which many Victorians liked to believe in and several mediums gained great fame during this time. The characters of Elizabeth Shelley and Professor Mortimer are very loosely based on the medium Florence Cook and the scientist Sir William Crookes.

Spiritualism is said to have begun with the American Fox sisters. They were Leah, Kate and Margaretta and claimed a spirit was the cause of mysterious noises in their family home in New York state in 1848. At the time, the sisters were aged between eleven and fourteen. Local interest in this 'spiritualist rapping' grew, and the sisters held their first public performance in Rochester in 1849. A year later, they held well-attended public seances in New York. Kate and Margaretta became famous mediums despite regular accusations of fraud. In 1888, Margaretta confessed that her 'powers' had been a fraud. However, she recanted her confession the following year.

In Britain, Florence Cook was a teenager when she claimed to be a medium in the 1870s; she materialised a spirit called Katie King. She regularly held seances and, although many people were doubtful of her abilities, she was endorsed by the scientist Sir William Crookes. Crookes was a chemist and physicist who was best known for his work on spectroscopy. His interest in spiritualism was said to have begun in the 1860s when he attended a seance to contact his dead brother. He studied the Fox sisters and concluded they were genuine. He also studied Florence Cook and the alleged Scottish medium Daniel Dunglas Home and published his findings in *Researches Into the Phenomena of Modern Spiritualism* in 1874. For a time, Crookes was the president of the Society for Psychical Research - an organisation which still exists today. Arthur Conan Doyle, the creator of the Sherlock Holmes, was also a member of the society. His belief in spiritualism is believed to have been strengthened after his younger brother died in the flu pandemic shortly after the First World War.

The development of Camden Town began in the eighteenth century and development grew rapidly after the construction of Regent's Canal and the railways. The good yards of the North Western Railway were a big employer in the area - coal and other raw materials from the north of England were unloaded here. Hundreds of workhorses were employed at Camden Goods Depot, so many that the depot even had its own horse hospital! The depot closed in the 1950s. Industry in Camden included gin distilling, food manufacturing, printing and piano manufacturing.

As industry declined in the area, it became popular with artists and musicians and developed a bohemian image in the 1960s. The Roundhouse – a former engine shed for the London and Birmingham Railway – became a popular music venue. The Rolling Stones, David Bowie, Led Zeppelin, Jimi

Hendrix, The Doors and Pink Floyd – among many others – played here early in their careers. These days Camden is a lively, eclectic place known for its live music, creative businesses and alternative culture.

Camden Square was built from the 1830s until the 1850s. Not long after its completion, some houses were demolished to make way for a railway tunnel beneath the square in the 1860s. The church which Penny visits, St Paul's, was demolished in the 1950s. The singer, Amy Winehouse lived in the square and a shrine to her is still maintained near her former home.

Highgate was a village outside London until it was swallowed by late nineteenth century development. It's now a wealthy suburb which has kept much of its character and green space.

Highgate Cemetery was laid out in the 1830s when London was running low on space to bury its dead. The cemetery is famous for its funerary architecture and the tombs of well-known people such as Karl Marx, George Eliot and Douglas Adams. Neglected after the Second World War, much of it is now overgrown and it's a fascinating, atmospheric place with a host of ghost stories attached to it. Such is the interest in the cemetery that guided tours are run each day.

Penny makes an evening journey to Highgate via Spaniard's Road – a lonely road which crosses Hampstead Heath. In the fog, she's relieved to finally see the lights of the famous Spaniards Inn, which has been a landmark for centuries. It was built in the sixteenth century and it's reported that highwaymen kept watch on the road from the inn. Dick Turpin is thought to have been one of them, as his father was purportedly the inn's landlord.

The first Theatre Royal on Drury Lane was built in the 1660s and the current building is the fourth one, it opened in 1812. Tunnels beneath the theatre apparently allowed King Charles II to sneak out and meet his mistress, Nell Gwynne, at the pub across the road. The Theatre Royal is also said to be the most haunted in the world, with the Grey Man, the Lavender Lady and the ghost of clown Joseph Grimaldi putting in spooky appearances.

The Royal Institution of Great Britain – where Penny meets Dr Corkhill - was founded in 1799 as an organisation for scientific education and research. The organisation has been housed in its grand building in Albemarle Street, Mayfair, ever since.

If *The Camden Spiritualist* is the first Penny Green book you've read, then you may find the following historical background interesting. It's compiled from the historical notes published in the previous books in the series:

Women journalists in the nineteenth century were not as scarce as people may think. In fact, they were numerous enough by 1898 for Arnold Bennett to write *Journalism for Women: A Practical Guide* in which he was keen to raise the standard of women's journalism:-

"The women-journalists as a body have faults... They seem to me to be traceable either to an imperfect development of the sense of order, or to a certain lack of self-control."

Eliza Linton became the first salaried female journalist in Britain when she began writing for *the Morning Chronicle* in 1851. She was a prolific writer and contributor to periodicals for many years including Charles Dickens' magazine *Household Words*. George Eliot – her real name was Mary Anne

Evans – is most famous for novels such as *Middlemarch*, however she also became assistant editor of *The Westminster Review* in 1852.

In the United States, Margaret Fuller became the *New York Tribune*'s first female editor in 1846. Intrepid journalist Nellie Bly worked in Mexico as a foreign correspondent for the *Pittsburgh Despatch* in the 1880s before writing for *New York World* and feigning insanity to go undercover and investigate reports of brutality at a New York asylum. Later, in 1889-90, she became a household name by setting a world record for travelling around the globe in seventy-two days.

The iconic circular Reading Room at the British Museum was in use from 1857 until 1997. During that time, it was also used as a filming location and has been referenced in many works of fiction. The Reading Room has been closed since 2014 but it's recently been announced that it will reopen and display some of the museum's permanent collections. It could be a while yet until we're able to step inside it but I'm looking forward to it!

The Museum Tavern, where Penny and James enjoy a drink, is a well-preserved Victorian pub opposite the British Museum. Although a pub was first built here in the eighteenth century much of the current pub (including its name) dates back to 1855. Celebrity drinkers here are said to have included Arthur Conan Doyle and Karl Marx.

Publishing began in Fleet Street in the 1500s and by the twentieth century the street was the hub of the British press. However, newspapers began moving away in the 1980s to bigger premises. Nowadays just a few publishers remain in Fleet Street but the many pubs and bars once frequented by journalists – including the pub Ye Olde Cheshire Cheese - are still popular with city workers.

Penny Green lives in Milton Street in Cripplegate which was one of the areas worst hit by bombing during the Blitz in the Second World War and few original streets remain. Milton Street was known as Grub Street in the eighteenth century and was famous as a home to impoverished writers at the time. The street had a long association with writers and was home to Anthony Trollope among many others. A small stretch of Milton Street remains but the 1960s Barbican development has been built over the bombed remains.

Plant hunting became an increasingly commercial enterprise as the nineteenth century progressed. Exotic plants fascinated Victorians and, if they were wealthy enough, they had their own glasshouses built to show them off. Plant hunters were employed by Kew Gardens, companies such as Veitch Nurseries or wealthy individuals to seek exotic specimens in places such as South America and the Himalayas. These plant hunters took great personal risks to collect their plants, and some perished on their travels.

The *Travels and Adventures of an Orchid Hunter* by Albert Millican is worth a read. Written in 1891, it documents his journeys in Colombia and shows how plant hunting became little short of pillaging. Some areas he travelled to had already lost their orchids to plant hunters and Millican himself spent several months felling 4,000 trees to collect 10,000 plants.

Even after all this plundering, many of the orchids didn't survive the trip across the Atlantic to Britain. Plant hunters were not always welcome: Millican had arrows fired at him as he navigated rivers, had his camp attacked one night and was eventually killed during a fight in a Colombian tavern.

My research for The Penny Green series has come from sources too numerous to list in detail, but the following books have been very useful: *A Brief History of Life in Victorian Britain* by Michael Patterson, *London in the Nineteenth Century* by Jerry White, *London in 1880* by Herbert Fry, *London a Travel Guide through Time* by Dr Matthew Green, *Women of the Press in Nineteenth-Century Britain* by Barbara Onslow, *A Very British Murder* by Lucy Worsley, *The Suspicions of Mr Whicher* by Kate Summerscale, *Journalism for Women: A Practical Guide* by Arnold Bennett, *Seventy Years a Showman* by Lord George Sanger, *Dottings of a Dosser* by Howard Goldsmid, *Travels and Adventures of an Orchid Hunter* by Albert Millican, *The Bitter Cry of Outcast London* by Andrew Mearns, *The Complete History of Jack the Ripper* by Philip Sugden, *The Necropolis Railway* by Andrew Martin, *The Diaries of Hannah Cullwick, Victorian Maidservant* edited by Liz Stanley, *Mrs Woolf & the Servants* by Alison Light, *Revelations of a Lady Detective* by William Stephens Hayward, *A is for Arsenic* by Kathryn Harkup, *In an Opium Factory* by Rudyard Kipling, *Drugging a Nation: The Story of China and the Opium Curse* by Samuel Merwin, *Confessions of an Opium Eater* by Thomas de Quincy, *The Pinkertons: The Detective Dynasty That Made History* by James D Horan, *The Napoleon of Crime* by Ben Macintyre and *The Code Book: The Secret History of Codes and Code-breaking* by Simon Singh, *Dying for Victorian Medicine, English Anatomy and its Trade in the Dead Poor* by Elizabeth T. Hurren, *Tales from the Workhouse – True Tales from the Depths of Poverty* by James Greenwood, Mary Higgs and others, *Sickness and Cruelty in the Workhouse - The True Story of a Victorian Workhouse Doctor* by Joseph Rogers, *Mord Em'ly* by William Pitt Ridge, *Alice Diamond And The Forty Elephants: Britain's First Female Crime Syndicate* by Brian Macdonald, *The Maul and the Pear Tree* by P.D. James, *The Five* by Hallie Rubenhold, *Sister Sleuths* by Nell Darby, *A Thousand Miles up the Nile* by Amelia Edwards, *Ancient Egypt:*

the Glory of the Pharaohs (audiobook) by David Angus, *Egypt: handbook for travellers, 1885 - 92* by Karl Baedeker, *Researches Into the Phenomena of Modern Spiritualism* by Sir William Crookes and *Dickens's Dictionary of London 1888*. The *British Newspaper Archive* is also an invaluable resource.

GET A FREE SHORT MYSTERY

❧

Want more of Penny Green? Sign up to my mailing list and I'll send you my short mystery *The Belgrave Square Murder*!

A wealthy businessman is found dead in Belgrave Square on a foggy November night. Was the motive robbery? Or something more personal? Penny Green tries to report on the case, but no one wants to cooperate. How can she investigate when there's so little to go on?

Visit my website for more details:
emilyorgan.com/the-belgrave-square-murder

Or scan the code on the following page:

GET A FREE SHORT MYSTERY

THANK YOU

Thank you for reading this Penny Green mystery, I hope you enjoyed it!

Would you like to know when I release new books? Here are some ways to stay updated:

- Join my mailing list and receive a free short mystery: *The Belgrave Square Murder:* emilyorgan.com/the-belgrave-square-murder
- Like my Facebook page: facebook.com/emilyorganwriter
- Follow me on Goodreads: goodreads.com/emily_organ
- Follow me on BookBub: bookbub.com/authors/emily-organ
- View my other books here: emilyorgan.com

And if you have a moment, I would be very grateful if you would leave a quick review online. Honest reviews of my books help other readers discover them too!

You can discover more about the Penny Green Series by scanning this code:

ALSO BY EMILY ORGAN

Augusta Peel Series:

Death in Soho
Murder in the Air
The Bloomsbury Murder
The Tower Bridge Murder
Death in Westminster
Murder on the Thames
The Baker Street Murders

Churchill & Pemberley Series:

Tragedy at Piddleton Hotel
Murder in Cold Mud
Puzzle in Poppleford Wood
Trouble in the Churchyard
Wheels of Peril
The Poisoned Peer
Fiasco at the Jam Factory
Disaster at the Christmas Dinner

Christmas Calamity at the Vicarage (novella)

Writing as Martha Bond

Lottie Sprigg Travels Mystery Series:

Murder in Venice
Murder in Paris
Murder in Cairo
Murder in Monaco
Murder in Vienna

Lottie Sprigg Country House Mystery Series:

Murder in the Library
Murder in the Grotto
Murder in the Maze
Murder in the Bay

Printed in Great Britain
by Amazon

42024126R00151